GODDESS

A HEROES AND VILLAINS NOVEL

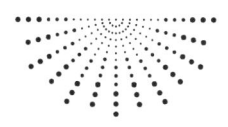

LIZA PENN

NATASHA LUXE

1
PERSEPHONE

I have carried many names.

Hela was what my mother called me, before she knew what types of power I would wield. Some of the mortals of Earth called me that. But there are other names for death: Anubis, the Morrigan, Izanami, Kala. At some point in time, someone has called me by each of these names.

But the name I choose for myself is Persephone.

The Greeks had a way with stories—they wove their worship into tales, they created poems and legends from the simplest things. Not always to explain or teach, as many of the early religions did. But to entertain. To become a story.

I like that. The Greeks knew that death was not so much an ending, but a new chapter to a new story.

I look out at my island—named Elysium, another Greek term. The place where heroes came after they died. Villains, too—anyone touched by the gods, fated to be epic.

It seemed an appropriate name for my realm. At the time, I had been hoping to make it truly idyllic, a place of rest and play, a separate realm for those with powers to find a safe haven.

But a part of me always knew, I think. I was never far from the memory of the threat that had killed my mother, ripped apart my own home world. Niberu.

Because as much as I wanted to reward the heroes —whether they be called Hero or Villain mattered not to me; they were all equally worthy in my eyes—as much as I appreciated them, I also knew…

He was coming. Niberu was always coming.

And if I made a playground for the powered heroes to frolic, if I pushed them to fulfill their darkest desires and revel in pleasure…

A part of it was a reward, surely.

But it was also to strengthen me.

I feed off feelings. I surround myself with high emotion—good emotion. Orgasms shudder through willing, satiated people here, and that sensation fills my veins with power. The rush of adrenaline as a desire is fulfilled zips through my veins like lightning. The thrill and release of fantasies come to life—and the fantasizer coming—strengthens my magic, roils in my muscles, vibrates through my body.

I do not need to participate in the fantasies to feel their effects. My psyche relishes in proximity.

But now, even though I am inches away from bodies pulsating in the throes of their deepest sexual fantasies…

It is not enough.

I curl my fingers into my palm.

I can *feel* the emotions spilling out all around me—lust is one of the strongest pulls for me, a reliable source of power. And yet now?

Nothing.

Or, at least, not enough.

"Something wrong, my queen?" The woman beside me has long, vivid red hair, and even though she speaks to me, I know most of her mind is elsewhere. Scarlet casts a dreamscape for the people on stage in my throne room, enabling them to live a fantasy while the rest of us watch reality.

"Don't call me that," I say pleasantly. My braids sweep over my shoulders, a dark contrast to her red.

Scarlet narrows her eyes at me, but she's too focused on the dreamscape she's made to really press me for answers. I should have known that she would guess something was wrong. I am closer to Scarlet than nearly any other mortal in this world.

But that doesn't mean she needs to know my secrets.

On stage, black wings burst forth in a powerful sweep. The audience gasps as Fallon throws his wings out wide. He circles the stage like a vulture.

I know—because I am connecting to everything on

this island, because I can see into Scarlet's dreamscape —that Fallon sees not my throne room with its stage designed to showcase people fucking. No, he sees his lover, Lillith, sprawled out on a bed of ferns. Lillith is here, too, her eyes milky as she writhes on stage, touching herself, her fingers slick with her own moisture.

This is the fantasy they wanted Scarlet to make for them—an innocent girl in a forest, playing with her pussy, while her dark lover watched from the skies. He gets off on "spying" on Lillith; she gets off on being seen—not just by him, peeping through dreamscape clouds—but on both of them knowing about the audience that watches them fuck.

Fallon swoops in circles, watching his beloved. His dick is hard, his hand pumping as Lillith fingers herself beneath him. When he comes, it falls across her body like hot rain, and she licks it up eagerly, her tongue flicking over her own skin, sucking away the drops.

Behind us, I hear moaning and longing, the wet sounds of other people getting themselves and each other off. This is my throne room—a palace of pleasure, a feast room of fucking. Every single one of the people here are brimming with lust and desire, their bodies singing with the satiated joy of orgasm, and it should be *filling* me up with power.

But it is not.

This is the most powerful my island has been. There are more people here at Elysium than ever before, each of them wrapped up in some high emotion. It's not just fucking—there's rage simmering under the Wreck three floors down as he spars with my brother, Thor. There's gluttony as Piper takes in the cocks of both Ari and Bryce, her dual lovers, in their private cabana. There's greed in the audience, begging for more even as Fallon and Lillith finish, and there's sloth, too, as people, spent, sink into the cushions of the booths, sliding into oblivion.

I have all the sins covered here.

Even...even pride.

That is my own.

And a bright, burning source of pride is down, far, far below, in the dungeons beneath my palace.

I shake my head, pushing the thought away. I have all the sins gathered here in Elysium, all the passions surging through my subjects, all the *power* they should bring...

And yet I am weaker now than I have been in a long time.

Too weak, I think, to face the one threat I must face, soon.

Niberu is coming.

And the only emotion that drowns out all the others, the only emotion I can focus on now, even though it weakens me, is fear.

2

MALCOLM

"I ordered the Martell L'Or," I say with a distasteful sniff at my cup. Floral earl grey tea.

She knows I *loathe* earl grey tea.

The guard blinks at me behind the pane of reinforced glass. The sheer blank look of stupidity on the man's face is enough to make me echo that distasteful sniff in his direction.

"Martell L'Or," I repeat. "Cognac? Brown liquid, typically stored in the opulent bottles placed high on bar shelves in establishments you likely do not frequent—"

"I know what cognac is," the guard snaps back. His cheeks flush red. "This is what you're getting. You don't get to *order* anything."

"Ah. I thought she was coming around to my presence? I have gotten some rewards for good behavior."

The guard's wrist comm beeps and a voice crackles

through. "Private, deliver the rations. Do not *speak* to the prisoner."

The guard's blush is vivid purple now. Without a further word, he scurries back down the hall.

I shove up from the chair placed before my small dining table and cross the cell in three strides—four strides long by three strides wide—only to see the guard pause before the locked door. He doesn't hit any buttons on this side—it only opens via a guard panel in the outer vestibule—but after a beat, I hear the airlock hiss, and the door swings open.

There—the guard panel, security footage showing me from various angles, a computer screen —

The door shuts.

I'm alone again.

Mostly.

I know she watches me. I know she listens. She may have my powers thoroughly locked down, but that's all the more reason I know she's spying on me—I can't do a damn thing to stop her.

I go back to the table and sit before the tray of food. "To call this *lunch* would be an insult. Do you remember when we dined at that seaside cafe in Greece? The luxurious hours of marinating in the sun while I fed you olives and fresh pasta…"

Today, I have a bowl of brothy soup, a hard roll of bread, that accursed cup of tea, and a plate of strawberries.

I lift one of the berries and bite through its sweet flesh.

"And then after," I grin at the berry, chewing slowly. "The secluded beach. The waves roaring on the rocks. I stripped you out of that black dress and bent you over right on the sand—"

A harsh *zap* jolts through my brain and I go careening forward, spilling the soup, shattering the tea cup on the floor.

When the pain settles, I hold in the position, gripping the table, face twisted in a grimace.

"So you are listening," I whisper, which earns me another zap.

This one lasts longer, burns deeper, and I can feel her intent in it. *Do not take liberties. Do not pretend you are a visitor here. You are a prisoner, and you have hurt me, and you have hurt our daughter, and you are a danger.*

And no one in the wide, wide world outside even cares that you are gone.

Whether it's Persephone or my own guilt, the image of Gwen pulses in my mind. Seeing my daughter here—what was it, weeks ago now?—outside my cell, knowing she would have the sight of me in this abysmal prison uniform forever seared to her subconscious was enough to make me almost apologize. And I did, to Gwen—but to Persephone?

There are no words in this language or any other that will sufficiently encapsulate all the things I need to say to her.

And the truth, the grotesque, roiling truth, is that I'm not sorry. The world trusted me with a mighty responsibility in being the CEO of Heroes Org. Persephone herself helped me attain that position; together, her as a goddess and me as the most powerful mesmer in history, we were meant to guide the world through the coming threat.

But no, I do not regret shucking our plan and casting a net of my control over Heroes Org. We needed protection; we needed action; we needed to *stop* Niberu.

We still need to stop Niberu.

Persephone is on her way towards that goal, at least. I hear little news, but what I can coerce the guards to tell me has been promising—she has managed to gather both her Villains *and* my Heroes so she now wields an army the likes of which the universe has never seen.

I never doubted her ability. That wasn't why I went rogue. And it wasn't about glory, either, or pride, as she's accused so often.

It's far simpler. Yet far more complex.

I sigh and push up from the table. Somehow, my uniform avoided the spilled food, but the floor is filthy now.

"I don't suppose I could get a replacement meal and a mop?" I ask, though I know the answer. Perhaps I could use one of my spare uniforms to clean—lord knows they're little better than rags anyway. Christ, I used to wear *Armani*—

A siren blares through the cell. At first I think it's Persephone punishing me again, but then lights begin to flash, and the panes of glass around my cell go from clear to black.

I run for the one that faces the hall. I see nothing through it now save for my own startled reflection, my gray hair in its usual sweep.

The sirens continue to blare.

"What is happening?" I shout at the glass. As though guards would bother to answer me if a true emergency threatens.

My stomach sinks. Hard.

Is it...

It can't be...

"What is *happening*?" I demand. Quieter now, my eyes lifted to the ceiling.

One word comes through.

One word that has my nerves flaring with heat, has my heart going cold and still in my chest.

"Niberu," Persephone whispers through my mind, and then even she goes black on me.

3

PERSEPHONE

I knew he was coming.

We all fucking knew he was coming.

The one force in the universe that is more reliable even than death is Niberu. Death can be averted. Niberu?

He comes straight for me. My home.

Just like last time.

Last time. On Asgard. I was so young then. I still had hope then. And Niberu came. And my home world was obliterated at my feet, all but a handful of survivors escaping to fight another day.

And now here he is again.

I know—I *know*—he's there in the armada attacking. I *feel* him, laughing, amused at the idea of demolishing Earth's only chance at fighting against the monster who devours worlds. But even as the first phaser blasts hit my island, even as I feel the loss of some of my followers dying under the blast, I know that he is far out of my reach, a tickle in the brain, just present enough to mock me.

Niberu hangs back, watching the destruction of my second home from afar.

I named this island Elysium, after a human concept of ancient heroes and gods finding sanctuary. This island is supposed to be the reward for the super-powered individuals who work for me, a reward with the dual purpose of feeding me their positive energy.

A sanctuary.

And it is aflame.

You fool, I think, and I hope Niberu can hear the thought I shoot towards his brain, *you should have killed me first.*

I feel his laughter.

Standing in my tower, I spread my arms wide, calling upon every resource in my soul to hold together that which is mine. My fingers curl, nails pointed up, arms tense, knuckles white as I pull from within myself the power I need.

Another round of phaser blasts.

But my shield holds.

My office door bursts open. "Persephone!" Scarlet shouts, skidding into the room. I'm barely conscious of her eyes widening when she sees me, but I know that she can sense the power I'm funneling through my body, every ounce of reserve, enough to block one attack.

But can I block more?

"Get here, *now*," Scarlet says into an earpiece. Moments later, my daughter, my precious daughter who I never wanted to have to fight, appears.

"Mom!" Her voice chokes on the word.

I am focused on my power, my shield, but Gwen is stronger than me—her emotions slam into me, both feeding me and draining me at the same moment. And through them, I see what she saw:

The entire south side of my island crumbled into the sea, nothing more than ash.

The foundation of the castle is cracked.

Some of my beloveds, caught in the crossfire. Killed. Blood and ash. Sorrow. Pain. Pain, pain, pain, pain, pain—

I rip my mind from my daughter's. "We must *focus!*" I snarl at her, unable to hold back the pain I've absorbed, the terror.

Gwen nods, eyes wide, lips slack with horror. Distantly, I'm aware of others in the room, but I focus on her.

Come here, I say, unable to do more than speak in her mind.

My knees buckle, and I drop to the stone floor. Another round of phaser blasts rattle my shield around my island.

Some of the firepower slips through. The eastern cabanas—Piper lives there, with her boys, Bryce and Ari—

They're not there now, Gwen whispers in my hand. She kneels behind me, resting her head against my shoulder, but she's not using me to support her body. Her touch is a way to funnel her power into me, to grant me more strength.

I see a flash, her vision, her memory. When the first phaser blast hit Elysium, Ari scooped Piper up, gave her to Bryce, who'd been training on the beach, and flew into the fight.

My heart soars at the vision I get from Gwen. Not the horrors of the war Niberu has brought to my literal door, but the heroics of my followers, rising as one to fight back. As I had hoped and worked for.

But my heart breaks, too.

Because I know they are not enough.

Ari, the All-American Man with super strength, is flagging. The Steel Soldier, my daughter's lover, is burning through his blasters and cannot sustain such a high level of combat. The Wreck, whose strength is enhanced with a power gem, is not here—he's with my brothers on a scouting mission, one I see now was misplaced. Fallon, sweet Fallon, has nothing but wings and his own courage to fight Niberu's plasma-shielded spaceships as they swoop down. The Doctor, the Watcher, so many more—they are fighting.

They have the same passion I have. To save this island.

To save this world.

But they are not enough.

Another blast.

I scream, and the shield I'd erected around the island shatters. I cannot hold it.

I am not enough.

Somewhere, far, far away, I feel a whisper of a voice I know. *You are.*

Gwen crouches in front of me, holding her hand out. She helps me to stand. "We can't give up," she says. There are tears in her eyes.

She knows.

Elysium is falling.

The floor shifts. Cracking rocks and screams of terror sweep through my mind.

"We have to evacuate!" Scarlet shouts.

I feel the crack in my castle. A phaser blast split through my shield, striking like lightning, all the way down into the sub-basements of my home.

But I am too weak, trying to hold it all together.

"Mom," Gwen says, trying to pull me away.

Get the others out, I tell her in her mind. I force all the emotion into the thought, the knowledge of the hundreds of scientists I've got working the underground labs, of the priceless data, of the Heroes and Villains in the healing chambers.

I've got the castle, I think to her.

Gwen nods, jaw tense. I'm exerting even more power than before, holding together the crumbling stones of my castle as well as a bubble shield around the island. The supers fighting against the ships firing phaser blasts buzz through my subconscious.

And Gwen, my perfect, powered daughter, *flies* through the castle, literally lifting up as many people as she can. Scarlet races out, using her mental powers to raise an alarm. Any powered person not fighting is working to help the non-powered people in the castle escape.

The floor beneath me cracks, the mortar splitting.

My whole body strains as I use every ounce of power I have to hold this building—this island—safe.

Is everyone out? I send my thought to Scarlet.

No, she says, desperate.

I cannot hold any longer.

I must. I must.

I'm blind and senseless to the world around me, even as I feel the floor beneath me shifting, my body falling. I am nothing but a power source to hold the walls together, the shield tight, a little longer, a little more.

But then I feel—

Warmth.

Strength.

Power. Love is stronger than fear, the strongest power there is. It floods through me.

I feel arms around me. *Gwen,* I think, but I don't hear her voice in my head.

No matter. I know this feeling.

This is love, pure and true.

And it is enough.

With a roar that boils from the depths of my soul, I funnel every bit of power I have left to *push*. The blast expels from me like a bubble, expanding and growing. It sweeps over the castle, phasing everyone still trapped inside to the outside. It rolls over my powered heroes, protecting them.

And then the force of this love, my love, all my power—it hits Niberu's attacking armada.

The ships are pushed—back, back, tumbling prow over aft, blown like petals on the wind. Several of them incinerate upon contact with my power; others crash into each other. A few escape.

But not enough to retaliate.

Drained, I feel my body sink down.

Strong arms catch me.

Carry me out of the debris of the castle that had been my home.

I am laid down in the grass.

My eyes flutter open.

Not Gwen, I think.

"No," Malcolm laughs. "Not our daughter."

My stomach churns, but there's not enough strength in me to vomit at his touch. Revulsion makes my lips snarl, though, and I curl up around myself. Acrid burning fills my nostrils; smoke clouds my vision.

"You," I spit. "How did you escape?"

Malcolm laughs again. "I think you mean, 'thank you for saving my life."

"I do not want your power," I grind out through clenched teeth. "I want *nothing* from you."

"Not even salvation at the end of the world?" Malcolm says. His voice is a whisper, so soft I'm not sure if he speaks aloud or directly in my mind.

I turn my face from his. "Not even then."

4
MALCOLM

We soar through the sky in one of the many jets Persephone has on Elysium.

Had on Elysium.

The sight of the island through the window shows a battlefield, great craters of explosions blackening the landscape, the once mighty castle reduced to ash and rubble. We are the last jet out—Persephone refused to leave until she knew that every soul had gotten to safety first.

Her self-preservation has never been strong.

And that is the simple, painful reason why I went rogue.

That is why, so many years ago now, I broke her heart, and mine, and Gwen's, and even though the ache is still as heavy now as it was then, I'd do it again.

"Sit down," I tell her as she paces the narrow hall of the jet. It's little better than a small cargo plane, with holsters along benches at the side. In these holsters now are those who remained with Persephone, and I note them with a cursory glance, weighing who put my wife's personal safety above their own. Many of them —Ari, Piper, Bryce, Lillith—give me fierce glares in return, looks half fury, half fear.

They have not forgiven me for the things I did that hurt them, too. The way I took over Heroes Org and used my mesmer abilities to control their actions. They will never forgive me.

I am well accustomed to that sensation.

"Sit *down*," I tell Persephone when she paces by me again, and this time I grab her wrist and tug.

She doesn't fight me.

She drops, limp, onto the bench next to me.

The ease of it sends a bolt of horror through me. She truly must be worn thin if she gave in that quickly.

Gwen, on Persephone's opposite side now, meets my eyes with a similar look of horror. Most of her life was spent watching the inferno that is my relationship with her mother; she knows better than most how incendiary we are to each other. And so in that moment, I know Gwen and I are both thinking the same thing:

She's hurt.

Persephone bats me away. "Do not touch me," she manages to say, and when my fingers leave her wrist, my heart seizes.

God, how I've missed her touch. The softness of her skin. The thrum of life beneath her veins.

"Perse," I whisper. "You're—"

"Do not *call me that*," she snaps, and finally, finally, she glares at me, rage and impatience, and my chest relaxes.

"You pushed yourself too hard, Mom," Gwen whispers. "Are you hurt?"

"No one can hurt me," she says with a pointed look at me. "I'm fine. What are our numbers?"

Gwen's lips flatten into a line. She glances over her shoulder, at Anthony—Anthony, who smartly has not met my eyes yet—before seeking out Scarlet further down the row.

They spend a few minutes filling Persephone in on the casualties. The wounded.

We're going to Scarlet's base, I hear, but I'm only half listening.

Persephone's mind is open to me.

My powers returned the moment a blast opened the prison wall and I got out, but even so, Persephone never lowers her own mental guard—least of all for me.

She wouldn't want me looking.

Then again, she's the most powerful force in the universe. If she didn't want me looking, she'd have her shields up.

Or maybe she's just too drained to keep them lifted.

Maybe that fight truly did hurt her, and she's hiding how wounded she is.

I hear her thoughts flash through her mind like gunfire. Each name of a life lost from Scarlet has memories flaring in Persephone's mind, pain, grief, such grief—but it only gets added to the mountain of too-similar emotion she holds deep within her, pain heaped atop pain for centuries.

I asked her once how it would work between us. Her, immortal; me, aging.

She told me she could give it up. That she would. If not for me, then for Gwen—in all her years, her lifetimes, she'd had no other children.

I don't know if she has given up her immortality yet.

I don't know yet if she's mortal.

The thought coupled with hearing her inner turmoil has me reaching for her hand again. I know how I used to comfort her and build her strength—love making, generally—but that is no longer an option.

So I settle for grabbing her hand, interlacing our fingers, squeezing hard when she flinches.

Scarlet keeps listing names.

Persephone's hand goes rigid in mine.

Let me help you, I push at her. *Use me. Take what you need. I am a tool at your disposal.*

That breaks through. I feel the realization sink into her mind. I am not someone she loves; I am not precious to her. I am a battery, I am a power source, I am the only thing keeping her from screaming.

After a beat, her fingers curl around my hand.

Scarlet's base is in a desert not far from the Heroes Org LA headquarters. Ari, Bryce, and the rest who hate me glare daggers at me as we descend as though I have strong armed them into revealing its location. Oh, of course I knew it was here; not only did All-American Man find it easily at my behest when he was trying to save his former fiancee, but Persephone had little secrets from me once upon a time.

I don't mention that.

I don't say anything, in fact, as the jet lands and movement takes over. Persephone unravels our hands and rushes off the plane, immediately asking about the survivors and wounded who arrived not long before us. Scarlet is on her heels; the rest of the plane's inhabitants push out ahead of me, and I let them, my eyes only on Persephone, who I watch weave her way through this massive arrival bay and vanish into a hall.

"Something's wrong with her."

I glance down to see Gwen beside me, the two of us on the end of the gangplank, her gaze locked where mine just was, on the hall that swallowed her mother.

A better father would lie. *Oh no, dear, she's just tired.*

"How long has she been like this?" I ask as I step into the landing bay. Gwen follows me, and the two of us walk towards the hall, sidestepping people rushing to unload supplies from the plane.

Gwen shrugs. "I'm not sure. A few weeks, maybe?" She looks up at me, and realization flashes in her eyes: that we're talking, that maybe we shouldn't be, that she's still furious with me for so many of the things I did.

My lips part to apologize. Again. Though I know it will come out insincere, and that's worse, isn't it?

So I stay silent.

"Did Niberu do something to her?" Gwen asks, and I let my breath out in a sigh.

It isn't forgiveness, but something tentative builds between my daughter and I. We both love Persephone, and that will link us for now.

"No," I tell her. Though honestly, *could* Niberu have done something to her? Poisoned her, weakened her, found a way to tap her powers and slowly drain them?

My hands fist. My vision goes red.

I have been uselessly locked away for so long. I thought that was for the best; I thought I had failed Persephone so spectacularly that the only place for me was out of her way.

What have I done, letting her bear this alone?

"Dad?" Gwen touches my shoulder.

We're in the hall of Scarlet's base now. Doors open around us, wounded from the attack filling every bed and free seat.

Persephone is just there, kneeling before someone

with a nasty burn on the side of their head, speaking low and calm to them.

I blink down at Gwen, my thoughts tumbling into themselves, shattering at the sight of the concern in her eyes.

Then I feel her.

Her delicate touch, prodding my mind, reading my thoughts with swift and gentle clarity.

The only reason I had my guards down was because of Persephone—I am an open book to her. I meant it; I am hers to take from what she needs.

I'd forgotten Gwen was just as powerful—even more so.

My face breaks into a huge grin. "My god, sweetheart, how'd you learn to do that?"

One corner of Gwen's lips tips up. "I've been training. It helps knowing what my powers actually are." It's a pointed jab at how I let her believe she had *my* powers growing up, when in reality, she was her mother through and through.

"Ah. Well, it's impressive." I'm trying to detract from what she might have seen.

She knows. But instead of addressing it, she just rolls her eyes. "You two are such idiots."

My eyebrows shoot up. "Excuse me? Who said you could speak to me like that?"

"Um, you did, when you decided to be a crappy dad."

"I—" I have nothing.

She knows. Again.

Ah. Having both a wife *and* a daughter who can read not only my thoughts, but my emotions, may prove disastrous for me in the end.

But I have my own weapons, too.

I push my powers at Gwen, only to find her mind locked down tight.

My grin returns. "Good girl," I say.

She jostles my shoulder.

"Hey—Scarlet needs help in room four." Anthony comes up behind Gwen and reaches for her waist. The moment he touches her, his eyes meet mine, and a look of well earned fear makes him pale.

"Dad, *stop*." Gwen turns to her...to Anthony. "Yeah, I'm coming."

I glare at Anthony as they walk away. He glances back once, swallows hard, mutters something I catch as *Jesus fucking Christ I hate that guy*, but the two of them are gone before I can respond.

A presence near me draws my focus, yanks me back around.

Persephone stands two feet from me, close enough that I can feel the energy palpitating from her—exhaustion and pain—but too far for me to touch her.

My eyes find hers. I am showing my desperation clearly, I know; I don't care.

"Our daughter," I start, common ground, "has terrible taste in men."

A ghost of a smile. But she shuts it down, her gaze level. "She takes after me in more ways than one."

My chest caves and I close the space between us. "Perse—"

"Make yourself useful," she tells me. She doesn't step away, though, and we are in each other's space, breathing the same air. "There are plenty of wounded. Help us here, be of service, or I will not bother locking you up next time."

Her eyes on mine are fire. Hatred.

Longing?

I prod her mind, feeling for her emotions—I am too bold with my powers—and there, yes, I feel in the ashes the embers of her love for me.

Those embers *burn*.

They are strong. Unyielding. She has buried them and tends to that burial daily, but in this moment of staring at each other, of inhaling one another, they flare, and I see a wince pinch her face, the faintest whimper sound in her throat.

"As you wish," I whisper. "My queen."

5

PERSEPHONE

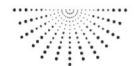

"They're gathering in the northern part of the Mojave Desert," Scarlet informs me as we stride through her base. The upper floor is usually host to various guests, but each room has been requisitioned as medical overflow currently.

The lower area of Scarlet's base houses her technological labs. She scans her eye to give us access to a room with a sunken floor and walls full of computer processors. A huge screen fills one wall, and a live satellite feed shows a vast expanse of desert.

"This area," Scarlet says, zooming the image in. "It's known as Death Valley."

"Fitting." The pale brown sand is speckled with black, and as the image becomes clearer, I make out the curved black lines of FX-700 star cruisers, each equipped with phaser blasters in the front and sleek silver firing cannons in the back. Combined, these two massive weapons can level a city block with one blast, and the solar-fuel cells lined up on the ridges of the ships mean that they have at least twenty or more shots before they need to reload. I scan the neat rows of attack ships quickly. They're laid out in even lines, troops waiting for the order to attack. Each unit is a hundred ships.

There are twenty—thirty—fifty units.

My vision goes black. This is more of an army than what took down Asgard.

Earth doesn't stand a chance.

There is always hope. I don't know where the words come from, but they whisper through my mind with a voice I don't want to hear. I push it away.

But I also square my shoulders, tighten my jaw.

"Incoming message," Scarlet says, tapping her ear piece. "From Heroes Org."

My brother, Loki, replaced Malcolm as head of the corporation that oversees super powered individuals on this world. "Bring him up," I say.

I expect Loki. But it's not his face that fills the screen. It's a human, some man with skin as white as a fish's belly and limpid eyes to match.

"Who are you?" I demand. "Where is—" I catch myself from using my brother's real name. "Lucas Gardson?"

"He is unavailable," the man says. He clearly attempts to muster some ounce of courage, but there is little to be had in such a feeble soul as his. "Lucas

Gardson has been relieved of duty with Heroes Org. I'm the acting CEO, and I demand that you remove those ships from the Mojave Desert."

"You sheer, imbecilic fool," I say, almost rendered speechless by his utter incompetence. They cast me as a Villain Queen merely because I had power and did not wish to use it to their benefit. And these decrepit men believe that any power that opposes their world is under my thumb? I can easily imagine Loki finally losing patience with this group of idiots who think they can order Niberu's space armada away.

And, because the idiot man still has not realized the truth of it all, I say, "Those are not my ships."

"I know they aren't," the man says. "But they said they'll go when you give them the…" He glances down, reading something. "The 'power gems,'" he says.

"You…" I blink, surprised that anyone human can be this stupid and still remember to breathe. "You think Niberu is going to just fly away if I hand him the power gems?"

"His terms were quite clear."

"Congratulations," I say sincerely, "you are the stupidest person I have ever spoken to, and I've been alive longer than humanity."

"How dare you accuse me like that," the man sputters.

"It was not an accusation," I state. "Merely a fact."

He opens his mouth to speak again, but I swipe my hand in his general direction, and Scarlet disconnects the video feed. "Bring me Loki," I say. Scarlet moves to a computer, typing rapidly.

A moment later, my brother's face fills the screen. "Sister," he says, the word almost a snarl, though his ire is not at me. Tension makes his neck taut, his eyes strained.

"You left Heroes Org?" I say.

"Obviously." Loki's in some sort of ship. A flash of green moves behind him—his lover, Rora, is piloting. "I took what heroes I could, those not under the thumb of politics," Loki continues. "We're on our way to you."

He means to Elysium, my island. The plan had always been to use it as a base, to unit all our forces there.

"Elysium is gone," I say. My voice doesn't crack, but from the way Loki's head whips up, his eyes searching mine, I know there must have been something in my tone to make my brother realize the depth of my words.

Had this been Thor, he would have offered his condolences, kind words of encouragement that this was merely a setback. Thor ever looked to the positive. But this is Loki. He says no empty words. He merely clenches his jaw, nodding once.

In his eyes, I see the truth I do not want to admit.

Niberu found Elysium because of *me.*

I am weaker now than I was before. No longer strong enough to protect the ones I love.

"Where are you?" he asks.

Scarlet sends him the coordinates, and Rora repositions the ship. "We'll be there soon," he says.

"Don't fly over Death Valley," I warn. Loki will look up the satellite feeds as he travels to us. He'll see what I saw.

He'll know the hopelessness of it all, the futility.

Loki's eyes flash with fury as he nods tightly to me. The video feed cuts out, replaced again with the live image of the ships gathered in Death Valley.

Waiting.

Ready to attack.

Niberu is toying with us. Elysium was a victory to him, and he knows it. He wants to see what desperate resources we can muster after losing the first battle, how easily it will be to swat us down before he destroys the entire planet.

"My queen," Scarlet says softly.

I shake my head, pushing her voice from my mind. They call me "queen," but I have never demanded the title of them. "Queen" is the title of a ruler. I never asked to be a ruler. I never attempted to lead.

They just followed me on their own.

I did not care, before. Follow me or not, the super powered beings that were drawn to my Elysium came and left of their own will; they bargained their services away for time on my island. And I won doubly—they both fulfilled the needs I had of their completed tasks as well as satiated the needs of my power reserves through their emotions, feeding me, strengthening me.

The weight of the well-being of them all falls to my shoulders, now. They are not merely faceless entities. They are *my* Ari, *my* Fallon, *my* Wreck.

My Gwen.

All mine.

If I am strong enough to protect them.

"Persephone," Scarlet says again, drawing my attention to her. "We need you at your strongest."

I close my eyes. "I'm trying."

Scarlet takes both my hands, pulling my attention to her. "No, I mean—we will know if Niberu rises to attack. Not only here," she nods to the screen, "but all my satellites are cued up. I have people watching. Here and elsewhere. We will know when he attacks."

When. Not if.

"And until then, you need to gather up all the reserves of power you have. We need you strong. We need you…full."

She gently pushes an image to my mind—her harem. It's sterile and white compared to my throne room of velvet-draped stone, but the purpose is the same. A place of pulsating bodies, of passions stoked, of ecstasy and orgasm.

A place for me to regain my strength.

The higher the positive emotions, the stronger I grow.

But it is true for the others as well. We have come out of a battle, a hard one bitterly lost, and emotions boil inside my soldiers. If I let them dwell in their current emotion—anxiety, grief, fear—that will override their senses. If I give them a release of emotion, the negative will pour at well. Opening the dam is a release of *all* their emotions, and it will serve them to not linger in their own fear and worries. It will serve them to let the flood pour out.

Pour into me, where I can turn every fear they have into power.

I nod. "Yes," I say, already stepping away. I know where to go. I feel Scarlet's power washing like a wave over the whole base—she's summoning every able-bodied person to the harem. Some have already gone, dispersed to recon missions to ensure Niberu has not infiltrated other areas of the world. My Gwen among them.

I take a deep breath. She will be fine. They will *all* be fine. I just need to, as Scarlet said, fill my reserves.

I take my time heading to the throne room. The anticipation is part of the thrill. And I want them all there, waiting for me. I want them on the cusp.

I send some mental feelers into the harem. They all need a release, not just me. High energy, high emotion, must have a release.

I rest my hand on the door leading to the harem. My cunt is wet already, desire twisting within me. Need.

No one denies me what I need.

Except Malcolm. The thought comes unbidden, but the truth of it has me weak in the knees. Malcolm was the first to deny me orgasm, to draw it out, to turn sex into a sweet punishment, to make the release something I had to work for.

To beg for.

His mesmer powers meant he could drive me just to the edge, the very edge, my body trembling with want, and then—

He would pull away. Take his cock from me, slide his fingers out of me, let the cold air bite at my body.

"Why do they call you Persephone?" he asked me once. "You are not a goddess of death, but of life."

"The French call an orgasm la petite mort," *I had told him. "The little death."*

It had amused him so—to call me the goddess of death, to know he meant something that wasn't deathlike at all.

"They all call me queen," I whisper to myself. But I am not. "I am a goddess."

I blink, and all my clothing evaporates. What prudes these mortals are. Clothing has never been needed.

I throw open the doors and stride inside. I do not need to look to know that every single person in the harem watches me, staring at my long legs as I march toward the stage. I feel the men grow hard, the women grow wet, just at the sight of me. The coil of desire each one of them feels inside winds around me, too.

I mount the stairs. I know they watch my ass. I know they see the glistening wetness between my legs.

I know they want to taste it. They—all of them—

they want to feel the silky moisture at the apex of my pussy, they want to slide their tongues into my cunt, they want to rub against my clit and feel my moans of pleasure.

I turn slowly. My eyes languidly roll over the panting people, each of them on edge, each of them begging me with their hard cocks and wet pussies to just please, please, *please* let me let them touch me.

My nipples are hard and puckered, the cool air prickling at my skin. I wait a little more, taking stock of my audience. Two dozen people heard the siren call of Scarlet's mental summons, twenty-four men, women, and other folk.

And there—in the back, his eyes hard, his cock harder—Malcolm. I should have known he would come. My pussy clenches. My mind cannot handle his presence, but my body wants him more than all the others. And it is my body that I must fill up now. Still, I push him away mentally. I may want him, but I cannot forgive him.

This harem is plain white, almost boring. Usually Scarlet is here, creating dreamscapes to add to the pleasure of the people present.

They do not need dreams.

They have me.

"I am a goddess," I announce, holding my arms out, my legs spread. "I am a goddess," I say, louder. "Come and worship me."

6
MALCOLM

My presence here is disruptive.

Make yourself useful, Persephone had said. *Or I will not bother locking you up next time.*

There is plenty to do among those tending the wounded. Or preparation—I know Gwen and Anthony are out scouting. I could easily fit myself into those plans.

But I am here.

I am here, and those around who know me as the mutinous former CEO of Heroes Org are torn between the wild eroticism that Persephone emits, and my scowling presence. They shift away from me, facing only Persephone, giving themselves over to the aura that palpitates off of her.

There is desperation in her aura.

Fear.

She is afraid.

She is afraid, and she is calling these mortals to worship her so she can reclaim her strength, and I know well that this is part of who she is and what she requires.

But that does not mean I enjoy it.

I watch, seething in a booth at the far corner of the room, as the first of the crowd approaches Persephone. A man takes one arm; a woman the other; and they hold her aloft as another man crawls between her legs, his face immediately burrowing into her warm, wet slit.

Persephone's head lulls back, and the air of the room deepens, ripens—those in the crowd begin to fuck each other, an orgy feeding off of her energy and in turn feeding her right back, so there is an air of manic to it all. Hands grab at bodies; fingers claw into skin; cocks drive home with vigor, and soon voices rise in mixed ecstasy and pain, and all around is the culmination of the previous battle's sensations being released in a protective shell of pleasure.

At the center of it all, Persephone lets herself hang suspended in the grip of her mortals, her body sheening with sweat as the man between her legs brings her to orgasm.

Her lips part. A dulcet cry comes from her mouth, but that is it.

Pathetic.

The man crawls away, slinks away more like,

knowing he failed her, knowing his futile attempts to worship her pussy were just that—*futile*.

Another replaces him, this woman at least beginning by kissing up Persephone's thighs, fingers playing with her nipples in whisper-soft tugs. Still, though, I see the frustration on Persephone's face.

This is not what she wanted.

The frantic sex around will serve to bolster her strength and powers—to a point. It will not give her what she *needs* though, not a way to truly recoup her strength.

I stand.

No one notices me; they have long given themselves over to their own pleasure.

How *dare* they.

How could they focus on themselves when they have a true goddess in their midst, one who is generously allowing them free rein of her glorious body? How can they not see they are so very inept, that every move they make is akin to a worm slinking through mud in comparison to what this goddess deserves?

My cock is rigid, pressing tight against the prison uniform I still wear, but I am more furious than anything. That fury grows when I see the resignation coat Persephone's face as the woman brings her to another disappointing orgasm—she will extricate herself from this orgy now and merely sit back and watch rather than tell them what she needs.

She fights for everyone else. She fights for whole worlds.

But she does not fight for herself.

I ascend the stage before she notices my presence. The man and woman holding her aloft flinch at the sight of me, but it is Persephone who dismisses them, pulling out of their grip and coming to her feet. The woman still kneeling before her wipes her mouth with the back of her hand and at least has the decency to bow her head as she dissolves into the still fucking crowd.

"You are not needed here," Persephone tells me, her voice rough.

She is utter perfection. Exactly as I remember. I fight to keep my eyes on hers, but her body is as worthy of worship as a goddess should be, deep, rich skin and voluptuous curves and heavy breasts.

My mouth waters.

I do nothing to bring up my mental shields. She has me. All of me.

"I would not be needed," I say, "if you would command them as you should."

Persephone's lips tighten into a line. "They give me what I need."

"Liar."

She flinches.

My rage spikes. She truly refuses to fight for herself. Even now, even here, in the middle of another Asgardian-level destruction, she would rather let these mortals take their pleasure instead of demanding her own.

I grab her arm. I have not touched her—roughly or gently—in far, far too long, and just the feel of her sweat-slick skin under my fingers has my cock throbbing.

"How long has it been since you needed to remind others of your safe word, hm?" My words are a growl, my own arousal mixed with fury. "How long since you have been delirious and unwound?"

Persephone shows me an image—her body in the throes of passion with a man and woman I vaguely recognize. The Raven and Lillith.

I sneer at her and take a threatening step closer. One of her feet slides back, the barest sign of retreat before she realizes what I made her do, and holds.

"You enjoyed yourself with them, did you?" I press, tightening my grip on her arm.

Persephone cocks one eyebrow. "More than I ever did with you."

I laugh. It is deep and ripping and only makes my cock ache more.

The look of determination on her face is destructive. Destructive because of what it will make me do to her.

I cannot draw full breath. I cannot formulate a coherent thought. All I know, all I am, is rage, rage on her behalf, rage for all the things she deserves and hasn't gotten.

By now, the crowd has noticed our tension. Many stare at us, paused in their ecstasy.

My eyes stay on Persephone's. My focus is ever on her, only on her, and I use my grip on her arm to pull her closer to me, where I run my nose along her shoulder, up her neck, inhaling her. She smells still of the sweetest nectar, the lushest breeze, heat and summer and life.

She smells of home.

I put my face just over hers. Her eyes stay on mine, and there is eagerness alongside her usual hatred.

She isn't pushing me away.

She isn't commanding me to leave.

That I know she would do, if she truly did not want me here. I am the sole exception in her world of self-flagellation—she will command no one except me.

Only now, in moments such as this, it is I who issues the commands.

"Pay attention," I shout at the crowd, my eyes still on Persephone's. "I will show you all how to properly worship a goddess."

7
PERSEPHONE

EVERYONE ELSE IN THE ROOM MELTS AWAY.

There is only me and him.

The others—they are no longer participants. They are observers. And while I feel a trickling of their anticipation feeding into my energy sources, it is nothing, *nothing* next to the tightly wound, pulsing desire at the core within me. These people are nothing more than an amuse-bouche.

Malcolm is the feast.

And I am starving.

I glare at him. He's still not touched me after his pronouncement. He's just...staring.

When my eyes meet his, he licks his lips.

Oh, fuck. He knows what I need, and he's going to give it to me...but the asshole's going to make me beg for it.

My eyes narrow. I radiate my displeasure with his smug look, but that just makes him smirk more.

Malcolm stalks me like an animal, a feral gleam in his eyes that has me wetter than I've been since...since I don't remember when.

You remember the safe word? he asks me in my mind. He doesn't need to ask, we both know it, but it's a reminder that I *am* safe.

I always am with him.

Honey, I reply. It was a play on his code name—the Hive, because he controlled the mindless little worker bees—but it's also a joke between us.

Some couples call each other sweet little names, endearments like darling, sugar, *honey.*

Not us.

We don't play like that.

As if to emphasize the point, Malcolm side-steps so he's behind me. I'm utterly bare, but this asshole still has his clothes on. I can feel the sharp bite of his belt buckle, the press of his cock through his pants against me. His clothing grates against my skin, offensive to the touch, but I say nothing.

I will not give him the satisfaction.

I feel a chuckle in his chest, against my back. His hard cock presses against my ass, it, too, angry at the zippered fly that acts as a barrier between us. Malcolm drapes a possessive arm from my shoulder down across my chest, so that his palm rests on the top of my left breast. He does not clutch at my breast or grab for my nipple like those mewling, weak offerings of the mortals who attempted to show me their reverence. His hand is lax, almost casual.

But I feel the taut muscles of his arm; I feel the way his body shakes with desire for me.

I let out a single sniff—inaudible, just a tiny puff of air through my nose, a simple, refreshing release of breath at the reminder of how much power I still have over this man.

In an instant, Malcolm's arm goes rigid. He shifts, gliding his rough touch to my shoulder and spinning me around on bare feet so that I face him. I see the tight clench of his jaw, the hard edge of his look, moments before his hands grab my shoulders, *hard*, fingers digging into my skin, a pain that grounds me.

That *reminds* me.

This isn't about me.

It's not about him.

It's about *us.*

Malcolm kicks at my legs, the hard side of his sole another bite against my skin. I spread wide. I can feel my lust dripping down my legs.

I'm tall, but so is he. We are at eye level. Our gazes lock. He holds my eyes—he doesn't blink or break eye contact even as he reaches for my pussy with one hand, driving three fingers into me without a moment of foreplay.

I don't need it. My cunt clenches around his fingers,

my body begging for more even as my eyes fill with glowering rage.

How dare he make me this wet? How fucking dare he still, after all this time, know exactly what I want? What I need?

His own gaze is filled with the same hate as mine. We are fire and oil, explosive and violent and never, ever supposed to be united.

But the burn is so sweet.

His fingers curl inside me, rubbing inside my inner walls, finding that spot—that aching, pulsing, needful spot—and he glides against it, pressing into it. Despite myself, a moan escapes my lips and my knees go weak.

The *instant* I express my pleasure, he withdraws.

His eyes still hold that same intense fury, but his lips smirk up, parting as he raises his fingers, letting his tongue flick out and lick the moisture from his skin.

And me? I'm left panting, my pussy quivering, my body aching for him to give me back his touch.

"You fucking asshole," I whisper, just loud enough for only him to hear.

"Are we doing ass play?" he asks, louder. "I wouldn't mind in the least, goddess. I can worship you from behind as well as from the front."

I open my mouth to protest—he will respect me, gods-be-damned—but he spins me about again, shooting his foot out so that I stumble and fall.

But he catches me.

As I knew he would.

Malcolm lowers me to my knees, ass up, toward him. I lift my head. Our audience watches, enraptured.

This is the difference. They all came to me on their knees. They cowered before my body, mewling like weak supplicants, begging for the chance to touch me.

Malcolm doesn't beg.

He takes.

And I give it, because that is what a goddess does. She gives.

I spread my legs wider, tilt my ass higher. Malcolm rewards me with a cupping touch of his hand as he spreads me open, sliding a finger from the base of my back and down, down, then through, into the eager, open, wetness of me.

He steps closer. Still clothed. This is part of his power play. He bares me, but hides himself. He spreads my cunt open so everyone can see how I'm dripping for him, but he keeps his cock safely behind his zippered fly.

Heat radiates off his body. He's so close now that I know if I could just take away his clothing, his cock would spring free and drive into me.

And so that's what I do.

In one quick, easy flick of my magic, I make his clothes disappear. His hard, hot, dripping cock falls forward, and—without needing to look or guide him—I slam my cunt against his cock, driving him all the way into me. A piercing shriek rips from my body at the same time he shouts, my pussy clenching around his cock, demanding it stay lodged inside of me.

Because that is also what a goddess does. She takes.

I use my knees to give me thrusting power. Malcolm is rooted to the floor, but I slam back into him, grinding my cunt against him, gripping his cock with the waves of my pleasure. My breasts swing free, my nipples so hard that the merest touch upon them would unravel me. My brains slide down my shoulders. All is sensation, all is touch, and I'm here, *I'm here*, feeling it all—him inside me, all the others boiling with lust as they watch, every single hot, ragged breath they take, it fills me—

But nothing fills me like Malcolm's cock.

He shifts on his heel, his dick twitching inside me. I gasp, going weak again, but he bends over me, supporting me with one arm.

"You can take from me all you want," he whispers, his voice a low growl, "but an orgasm can only be *given*."

I whimper.

Malcolm shifts again, almost withdrawing from me despite the way my inner walls clench at him. He gets on his knees, sitting back on his ass and shifting me so that I'm on top of him. It must be painful, but we both know—there is pleasure in the pain.

My body is splayed over his, my legs wide, my cunt pierced by his cock as he sits back. The audience sees me, spread wide, open before them, and already their cum spurts out, their bodies hunch in release, their moans fill the room.

They have their little deaths. I am, after all, the goddess of death.

But me? I have none of that.

Not yet.

Not until Malcolm gives it to me.

One of his hands grabs at my breasts, using the force to push me back against his chest, my body arcing out. I feel unhinged, as if he'll slip away from me, but he thrusts up, pressing his cock into me at an angle that immediately finds the spot where all my lust coils in tight tension. His other hand slides down, down, finding the place where we meet. He toys with his own balls a moment, a deep, rumbling laugh in his chest as I squirm, begging him with my dripping cunt to finally give me the release I need.

And his fingers go to my clit. There is no gentle swirl—he presses, *hard*, right on that sensitive bud, grinding into me in a way that makes me scream in both pain and pleasure, and with that touch, that driving insistence of *him* at my clit—I come apart, my body seizing in pleasure and then unwinding into boneless release even as his cock pumps hot inside me.

HE SLIDES me off him gently, careful with me, showing me the reverence he denied me before. His legs splay out, and he cradles my body with his. It is warm here, and safe, and—

I have never felt better.

All this time, my power was drained of me. Trying to protect everyone, trying to hold it all together—and yet no one, not a single person, could fuck me well enough to make me feel...feel *this.* This safe, this strong.

Because I do feel strong.

I feel like I could pluck Niberu from the sky and crush him between my thumb and finger.

"You could, my goddess," Malcolm whispers to me.

I push him from my thoughts. Instead, I reach out with my power, testing my reserves. I can sense each and every one of my people here on Scarlet's base. I can sense Scarlet herself—we were fucking in her harem, and she experienced an orgasm with us, even if she hadn't been in the same room. Her release adds to my power, already overflowing.

I reach further. There is Loki, in a ship, heading to us. Further, further. There is the Wreck, with the power gem he wields, strapped to his chest with sterlinium armor. I sense the other power gem, the one I have, carefully protected where I left it.

And I sense the third gem.

Niberu's gem, the last he has, but powerful enough to wipe off all life on this planet.

I sense them all. I feel their resonance. I feel their power.

Oh fuck, I think. One good fucking from Malcolm and that's how strong I get? Fuck.

I told you I know how to properly worship you, Malcolm whispers in my mind. His body is still carefully holding mine, but the mental voice he uses is full of mockery, teasing me with the knowledge of just how well he pleased me.

Get out of my head, I growl back.

As long as I get to stay inside your cunt. His hand, which had been casually draped over my pussy, twitches, one finger sliding into me.

Who needs power gems? I can just let him fuck me into power. I'm still wet, my body still vibrating for more, more, more.

I shift around to my knees, ready to let him worship me again.

But then I hear the alarm.

8
MALCOLM

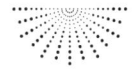

I race through the halls behind Persephone, tugging back on that damned prison uniform as she straightens her gown. The two of us are flushed and breathless—now from not only sex, but fear.

Scarlet appears beside Persephone. "They just got back— their comms were blown out— we didn't know until—"

"*Where is she?*" It is a growl. It is a command. It comes from the very pit of me, the core of my being, and both Scarlet and Persephone look back at me, Scarlet with pure terror—she and her Watcher know intimately the lengths I will go to in order to protect things that are *mine*—and Persephone with a look of surprising softness.

I have taken charge. I have taken this weight from her with one question, one absolute tone.

Scarlet points as we continue half running, half

scrambling through her endless halls. "Here, here, she's—"

I shove her aside and kick into the door.

There, in a stark white room, on a tasteless medical bed, is my daughter, unconscious.

Next to her, clinging to her hand so his knuckles are white, is Anthony Stern.

He launches to his feet at my arrival, but he doesn't relinquish his grip on her, doesn't make way for Persephone and I to take charge over Gwen.

The look I give him is withering.

The power I shoot at his brain is lethal.

Anthony crumbles to his knees with a garbled cry.

"Malcolm." Persephone says my name, even, but I hear the restrain behind it. She's barely holding herself together; I'm not so successful. "He didn't do this."

"No. But he should have *prevented* it."

Anthony gasps as I release my grip on him.

He still hasn't let go of Gwen's hand.

The smallest spark of admiration lights in my chest, but I smother it when he looks up at me, bloodshot, tear-stained eyes, as if he has any right to feel remorse for letting *my daughter* come to harm while on a mission with her. That is the role he has taken on, is it not? Her *protector*, her *lover*? And this is what he lets it come to?

Gwen hasn't stirred, but the rise and fall of her chest along with the beeping of a heart monitor tells me she is alive.

That is all that is keeping me from painting the walls with Anthony Stern's blood.

"What happened?" The question slips between my gritted teeth.

"We got too close," Anthony says. His eyes flick to Gwen. "She thought she could pinpoint the exact location of Niberu in his encampment, his gem, any traps. But they spotted us. And—" Anthony's other hand lifts the thin white blanket to reveal a gash on Gwen's side, her skin mottled, blood congealed, a crude battlefield bandage the only thing keeping her together.

"*SCARLET!*" I scream both out loud and through all the minds in the vicinity until that woman has no choice but to rush in. She comes with Watcher and a handful of her medical team.

"They were tending others," she says to Persephone, a winded, weak excuse. "I pulled them out of surgery as soon as—"

"If my daughter is still bleeding out on this godforsaken bed in the next five minutes," I start, "I will level every living soul in this compound and hand Niberu his victory."

It is only a half truth.

I will kill them all.

But I will never let Niberu be victorious, not while I draw breath.

Persephone's eyes hold on mine, reading the truth I show only to her.

She does nothing to refute my claim, and Scarlet

and her team spring into action, albeit stiff and casting furtive glances my way, no doubt wondering why Persephone tolerates my traitorous presence.

For them, Anthony steps aside, letting them work, but he lingers behind, terror graying his features. I see now that he's wounded as well, a cut on his hairline, and he removed the breastplate of his Steel Soldier uniform, showing a heavy bruise that starts on his shoulder and vanishes under a sweaty white tank top.

Good.

Let him suffer.

"Malcolm." Persephone takes my wrist in her hand and tugs. "Come. You are distracting them."

"I am making sure they know what is at stake should they let my daughter die." The words snap out of me, and the last one hangs before me, *die*.

Die.

I see Gwen on that bed, unconscious, her face tipped towards me, cheeks dirtied and her hair dusted with rocks and debris from whatever blast tore through her side.

Die.

I see all the times throughout her life when she was injured. Falls from bikes. Daring climbs on playsets only to tumble down onto gravel. Friends throughout her schooling who treated her badly and left her in tears. Boys, too, who broke her heart. I flattened playsets once I got her home safely; I struck the fear of god into friends and boys alike; I made sure anything that ever hurt her felt the brunt of repercussion, as if fate would learn quickly that harming Gwen Odyssey would do nothing but beget a worse pain onto the world.

All those moments congeal with this one, and though the other pains were the center of my world at the times they happened, they are blips compared to this threat, and I would trade anything to have a hundred heartbreaks over watching a medical team cut through my daughter's armor and use tweezers to pick rubble from her flesh.

Scarlet cries out first. She grabs her temples and curves into herself, screeching to the floor; Watcher grabs her, his yellow eyes flashing up to me before darting away in fear.

A nurse screams next. A man beside her too. Anthony again—

"Malcolm!" Persephone seizes my arm. Immediately, the screaming quiets, confusion and terror settling over the room in a thick fog.

"Go," Persephone tells me as she pushes me for the door.

I let her lead me out, rationale bidding me to comply. If I murder the medical team, they cannot help Gwen.

But once Persephone gets me into the hall and the door shuts us off from our daughter, the tension flies from my shoulders, the anger burns up in my chest.

I gasp, lungs aching, and blink down at

Persephone—

She's crying.

She's *crying*.

I was so focused on Gwen— so focused on my own pain over this situation—

Immediately, I sweep Persephone into my arms. I do not yet know where her feelings lie, even after our performance in the harem—but in this moment, I take charge again, demanding she accept my comfort.

She does. Her arms thread around my neck and she lets me hold her and Christ, a whole section of my heart snaps back into place, instantaneously healed.

My eyes stay on the door to Gwen's room.

"He hurt her," Persephone whispers into the slope of my shoulder.

My grip tightens on her.

I cannot put words to what I feel. An overwhelming, all-encompassing tear of *no*. No, he will not hurt her again; no, he will not hurt Persephone, either; no, I will not allow it, I will not *allow it*—

But I stifle that rage and breathe Persephone in, feeling the weight of her body, the inhale and exhale of her life against me.

My eyes close.

We are tired and terrified and angry.

But in this moment, we are together, and our daughter is near, and she *will* be all right; and I am, impossibly, stupidly, starting to feel something like whole again.

9

PERSEPHONE

M<small>ALCOM'S RAGE BOILS, HOT AND VIOLENT, NEAR</small>-chaotic in the way he lashes out.

My rage *burns*, slow and spreading, all-consuming. It is not a wildfire with crackling ash and breaking timbers; it burns like the heat of the sun, incandescent and ruthless, devouring but silent.

I lead Malcolm away from the room where the medics are working on my—*our*—Gwen. I understand his desire to destroy but not these workers, not yet.

Niberu deserves all our rage.

I weave my hands in Malcolm's, rest my forehead against his. We both close our eyes. For a moment, all we do is feel each other's mutual rage.

And then I push a memory from my mind into his.

A<small>SGARD</small>. *The night before Niberu destroyed my home planet.*

. . .

I FEEL Malcolm question this gift of my thoughts. I have been closed off from him for too long.

He knows what those last days on Asgard were like, the way Niberu betrayed my parents and destroyed my home world. He knows, because I had to show this to him to make him fully grasp the depths of the danger Earth was in.

Ironically, I wonder if my showing those memories to him, before, were what made him go rogue. I showed him the truth, and he reacted...poorly to it. But he had intentions I sympathized with, at least.

Besides, I have been called a Villain long enough to appreciate that most are given the label merely because they chose actions that disagreed with men who would call themselves Hero.

But now, in this moment, as our daughter lies grievously injured, I give Malcolm another memory.

I give him the memory I had of Niberu. Not the conquering tyrant—no, the man.

"THEY SAY YOUR BROTHERS ARE GODS." Niberu is half-drunk on Asgardian wine, but while his body is relaxed, his eyes are sharp.

I give him a little shrug. I know of his power, his reputation. He has come to my father with the intention of negotiating a peace between our planet and his army, but few believe that peace is something that can actually be achieved.

"And they say you are a goddess." Niberu speaks without question. He knows the answer. But he wants to hear me confirm it.

"They say that."

"The goddess of death."

"That is what they say."

Niberu pushes off the chair he'd been sprawled in. Not half-drunk. Not drunk at all. His steps are sure, his movements decisive.

"Death, hm?" He says the word as if it excites him.

"Death is too simple a term," I say, careful to keep my calm but also my distance. "I represent change. To many, that is a type of death."

Niberu's face is blank for a moment, then his lips curve up. Not a smile—at least not one that reaches his eyes.

"Change—I see. Such as if a virgin were to be thoroughly fucked—that would be the death of the virgin, but the birth of a whore." His eyes rake over my body—down and then up and then down again—purposefully lingering his gaze so that I can fully understand his intent.

"You forget," I say coldly. "I am not merely a goddess. I am also a princess of Asgard. And a woman—neither a virgin nor a whore, but a woman who needs nothing less than your approval."

Niberu laughs. "It's not approval you need from me. It's salvation." My blood runs cold as he leans forward. "Come with me, goddess of death. Let me show you what death can really do."

I wondered then—did he want me? The evidence of his lust strained against his trousers, burned his eyes to molten embers, made his knuckles whiten in bunched fists. But did he want me—or the idea that I represented death? His lust wasn't aimed at my body, but at my powers, my godhood.

This was a man in love with death itself.

"THAT WAS the moment I decided to steal the power gems," I whisper, my eyes still closed as I press my head against Malcolm's. "That was the moment I realized there was never any hope that Niberu would ever do anything more than destroy. He *loved* death. Destroying worlds is an aphrodisiac to him."

"The way he looked at you..." Malcolm's voice was a low growl. "He hurts my daughter; he threatened you."

I open my eyes and stare into his. His pupils are dilated; his jaw set. "My baby girl, my Gwen—" His voice cracks.

I have never loved him more.

Malcolm has made mistakes—terrible ones. He treated other Heroes as disposable means to an end.

But the end he strove for was an end to Niberu.

The world he was trying to save was mine, mine and Gwen's.

That's the difference between Niberu and Malcolm.

Niberu wanted to watch the world burn. Malcolm didn't care if the world burned or not—not as long as he protected his wife and daughter.

"You were right before," I tell him, my voice still low. "My powers have been faltering. But just before—" I cannot bring myself to say *"Just before Gwen was injured,"* but the words hang between us, a heavy stone of grief. "Just before," I continue, "that moment with you…"

"My love," Malcolm says, a little smirk on his lips. "Are you telling me that you need me to fuck you into full power?"

I bite my lip. It's not just fucking—it's high emotion. Fucking is the quickest, easiest way to a surge of emotional energy.

But there is nothing stronger than love.

And fucking while in love?

That's the power I need.

10

MALCOLM

She is asking me to fuck her.

For years, I have dreamed of this moment occurring again.

I never thought I would get it back.

But here it is, and all I can do is reach out and stroke my hand down her cheek, cup her jaw in my palm.

"What happens," I start, mouth dry, "when you are at your full power?"

Persephone's glistening eyes sharpen. She was already in the throes of delirium, of fucking; that I would refuse or question her is absurd.

"What do you mean?" Her voice is clipped. "I will face him. I will fight him. And I *will* defeat him."

"How?" My grip on her jaw dips to her neck, and I hold her there, hold her with me. "By facing him yourself? Him, and the army he has amassed, and the power stone he will use—"

"I have a power stone too. Two, actually."

"Your immortality will not protect you from being killed in battle."

Persephone's lips draw into a thin line. Something flashes in her eyes that I can't interpret, and when I push at her mind, she has me locked out again.

Does she still have her immortality?

Has she given it up? For Gwen. Not for me.

I growl at her, my control slipping, fraying, and I am still wound with terror over Gwen, over Persephone too, with no outlet left but *her*.

"You would face Niberu no matter the end it brought to you," I manage through my clenched teeth.

Persephone gives me a blank look. A look that says *Of course, what other way is there?*

My honorable goddess.

My self-sacrificial queen.

My stubborn love, who wouldn't hesitate to hurl her body into any danger if it meant saving us.

"That doesn't work for me," I tell her.

She blinks.

Understanding dawns on her face. Maybe it's my unfiltered look of rage. Maybe it's the way I grip her neck, a reminder of my restrained power. Maybe it's the way I open my mind to her, and allow her to see into me, all of me, the reasons that have fueled my every action over the past years:

The first image of Persephone holding our infant daughter, her face sweaty from childbirth, but the look in her eyes one of undeniable love; and Gwen in her arms, so tiny and perfect and soft. A dozen overlapping images of the two of them over the years, my girls. The three of us, in rare moments of cohesion, laughing together.

I will keep Persephone alive.

I will keep Gwen alive.

Nothing else has mattered. No one else has mattered. Not even myself. Not even the world.

The full brunt of my love for Persephone, for Gwen, pours forth, and I watch as Persephone basks in it, the emotion filling her up just as thoroughly as our fucking. Her skin starts to glow softly, a delicate gray light, and her eyes tear, soften, until she reaches up and loops her fingers around my wrist.

"Malcolm," she gasps my name, and my chest starts to crack.

"I will not lose you," I tell her. No one has ever said anything more true. "I will not lose Gwen. I will not let you destroy yourself for peace, Persephone, even if that means I have to restrain you myself."

She smirks.

It falls quickly.

"If it comes down to stopping Niberu or saving me," Persephone starts, and I suck in a breath, intending to counter her; she puts her fingers over my lips, "you will choose to stop Niberu. You will choose it because my life will have been forfeit otherwise. Everything I have suffered, everything I have done, will be lost if the moment comes, and he survives."

"No," I say around her fingers. "I will choose you. Always."

Her eyes pinch. The softness of my love for her and our daughter cannot withstand *this*; it has never been enough to get us past *here*, our mountainous stubbornness, this uncrossable canyon that separates us.

She will fight for the universe.

I will fight for her.

And here, now, those two things conflict.

"I told you," Persephone says, her voice level, "to be useful. If you step in my way, I will see you removed. You know you are no match for me, Malcolm."

My nostrils flare.

We have had such conversations before. Not of this, not so direct; but disagreements where I refused to budge and she refused to break and we went away in a storm.

Now, especially, I do not want that. I know she will need all the strength she can get if she is to survive fighting Niberu. She will face him no matter what I do, and there is still a chance that he will fall without her needing to intervene so drastically.

So I bend forward and kiss her. It is not a soft kiss, no gentle nip in this empty hall; our lips meet in bruising clash and I delve my tongue into her mouth, seeking, demanding.

"Then I will be useful," I say.

My hand is still on her neck; I tighten my grip and begin walking her backwards, up the hall.

Her eyes meet mine, but I keep our faces close, our breaths mingled, sharp and furious and terrified and manic. In a few moments, we're back at the door to the harem. I kick through it, and the attention of the room pulls to us.

It hasn't been but half an hour since she and I held this room in rapture, but more people are here now. I can feel their minds beating—the allies Persephone has built, minus Stern, our daughter, and her brothers with their women.

Others are present though. Others who seethe with fury at the sight of me, as always. The mood of the room shifts when we enter, Persephone and I focused wholly on one another, and the tone of fear—*Gwen was attacked; did you hear what happened; Niberu grows bold* —shrivels and shrinks into one of curiosity. Wonder.

Hope.

We give them a point to fixate on. Their leader, their queen, being driven backwards across the room by her neck, going willingly—they know she would cast me off if she did not wish this. And me, a devilish, deranged look on my face as I get to the dead center of the room, the space where a dais is empty now, and push Persephone down on top of it.

War is coming.

My love will be at the center of it.

So I will give her what she needs, as much as she needs, and if she makes a shield of herself between Niberu and the world, I will destroy myself to push her aside.

I understand her at that moment. Her selflessness.

I am selfless in a way too.

The thought makes me chuckle; no one would *ever* describe me as selfless. But for Persephone and Gwen, I am.

Persephone props onto her elbows, staring up at me. She is slack, waiting. *Worship me*, that posture says. *Give me what I need*.

I stand above her and begin stripping out of that accursed prison uniform. There's a gasp in the crowd; I can feel a pulse of shock, some satisfaction. It is debasing, what I'm doing. It gives Persephone control though I am the one moving and choosing to do this. And when I am naked before her, my cock hard and long before me, the tip glistening in the lowlight of the harem, the tension of the room could snap with one word.

All these people who hate me, all the lives I ruined and toyed with, all are now staring at me, bare. And though I know the sight is impressive—I was able to keep some of my muscle definition in Persephone's prison cell, and though I am older than most of the people here, I could out-bench-press everyone at Heroes Org, save for All-American Man.

Biceps flexing, I bend down before Persephone,

going to my knees between her legs. Her thin, gauzy dress parts as I slide my fingers up her knees, her thighs, letting the material fall back.

There are others in this room. Dozens. She would have this no other way.

But now, I see only her. I bar my mind to everyone else, focused solely on her pleasure, the rises and pulses of her body.

The velvet soft skin at the apex of her thighs is damp still from our previous fucking. This will not be so rough, though; this will be drawn out, gentle, a physical representation of the love she felt pouring out of me.

Her skirt falls back fully, exposing her plump pussy for me, the hair shorn close and thin. I run my thumbs down her lips, back up, parting the folds until her clitoris bulges forth. The motion makes her suck in a breath, but her eyes on me are still full of unspoken command.

Worship me. Give me what I need.

She knows I will stop her when it matters most. She knows I am her most dangerous enemy in that regard: I will keep her from stopping Niberu.

But she bends back, her head tipping up, her eyes closing, and she gives me free rein of her body.

I dip down and bury my face in her folds, running one long lick from her ass up through her pussy and ending at her clit. I can taste myself on her still and my cock gives a knowing twitch, but I'm lost quickly in the feel of her clit in my mouth. The soft, tender bud grows hard and larger under the ministrations of my tongue, swirling around and prodding gently in a building dance. Persephone's breathing quickens; I feel the pulse in her thighs speeding up too. And so I know we are both rising together as I make love to her clit with my mouth.

She comes—it will be the first of many—with a satisfied whimper, but I pull her clit into my mouth as she does, sucking hard to prolong the ecstasy. Her noise pitches, crooning, and still I suck, adding three fingers that plunge into her tight, warm pussy and bend to find that more sensitive spot.

My sucking intensifies; she will come again, she will come because of me, she will come *now*.

I pump my fingers and she cries out, her body arching backwards, breasts pushing up to the ceiling.

Two orgasms would make most back off—not me. Two is not enough. I relax the suction and lick her clit again, fast and crazed, a man possessed, alternating with rapid pumps of my fingers against her G-spot. Persephone writhes and when I reach my free hand up to pin her stomach to the dais, I see others there already—one holding her arm down and playing with her nipple, another pinning her opposite arm and sucking on her neck.

Faster, faster, my tongue and fingers in tandem, until Persephone screams, her body vibrating with sensation and pleasure and that too-raw wash of orgasm stacked atop orgasm. Around us, those holding her are being fucked by their partners, and throughout the room, the orgy has a feeling of determination now. Preparation. They are following our lead. They are fortifying themselves.

Only now do I crawl up Persephone's body and line my cock up at her entrance. Her juices drop down her slit, gushing around my already wet cock as I slowly, slowly, slide into her, letting her warmth envelope me in steady, dizzying increments.

Persephone bucks against those holding her. Her eyes open, bleary, and she finds me, panting and sweat-slicked.

I shove all the way into her.

She moans, her legs kicking up to lock around my hips, anchoring on me.

Yes, I push at her. *I am your anchor. I am your rock.*

My hips thrust, arching up with every shove to hit her G-spot, rubbed tender from my fingers. The added rawness has her eyes rolling shut again, utterly succumbed to the feel of our union. But I know she is drawing on the sensations around us too, the fucking of her allies. I don't have to have her powers to feel the strength in it; these people are not just lost in the throes of desire, they are bonded in the same way I am bonded to Persephone.

I slow my thrusts, speed them up, slow them again, toying with us both, dragging this out. We flip around so she is on her knees before me and I can plunge ever deeper, and that has us both making desperate, keening noises that fill this large chamber. And as my long-awaited orgasm washes over me, Persephone comes again—the fifth, sixth, maybe seventh time—and we cry out together, our sweat-slick bodies grasping feverishly at each other, more unified and more molded together than we have ever let ourselves be.

Because even though we are opposed, we are one.

And it is that oneness that will either be our salvation or our destruction.

11
PERSEPHONE

It is sweet, the way he focuses entirely on me.

It is hot, the way he fucks me into oblivion.

But this...this has always been about more than just us.

My body is limp—I'm satiated by his love-making. And love *is* the most powerful of the emotions that can fuel my power.

But beyond love, I need *all* the high emotions. I can feel the people watching us, and it is a tantalizing flirtation with the power they can offer. I do not want to dance and dip into these heightened senses, though—I want to swim in them. I want to bathe in them.

Malcolm is the first to sense my desire. He smirks—he knows how well-pleased my body is, but he understands. He steps back, motioning for Scarlet, who has, somehow, arrived without my notice.

Your daughter will be fine, she tells me in my mind. *Now let's ensure you have everything you need.*

Scarlet mounts the dais, waving her hand. A hidden panel in the floor rises automatically, revealing an assortment of toys. Another wave of her hand. Another panel rises—no, not a panel.

A body-sized X-shaped cross, with padded restraints.

The Saint Andrew's cross looms on the stage. With a nod to Scarlet, Malcolm scoops my body up and carries me to the cross. I send my clothes away, and he presses my bare ass against the point where the cross meets. Malcolm leans his body against mine, pressing me to the cross. His cock is hard again, and from the smirk on his lips, I know exactly what he wants.

His legs kick mine open. Scarlet kneels down, restraining my legs against the two lower parts of the cross, while Malcolm roughly pushes my arms up, snapping the buckles against my wrist.

I know your safe word, he tells me in my mind. *You need only think it, and you'll be free.*

I don't want to be free, I tell him. *I want to be worshipped.*

That, we can do.

He thrusts up, his cock easily sliding into my wet pussy. My legs twitch, wanting to close around him, but I'm splayed open, my legs and arms open and tightly restrained. I try to buck my hips up against him, craving his dick, but I feel Scarlet's warm hands around my waist, then a silk band binding my torso to the cross.

Malcolm slides out of me, purposefully twitching up so his cock hits my swollen clit. I gasp, but my body is so firmly constrained that I can do nothing else. He steps back, his eyes raking over my body. I am bare, and I am open. Cool air kisses my wet cunt; my nipples are hard and pointed, my breasts splayed. Scarlet touches a button, and the cross rack raises and tilts so that my cunt is eye-level with Malcolm.

He licks his lips, salivating at the sight of me. But rather than do anything, Malcolm whirls around. "Well?" he booms, his voice loud and echoing throughout Scarlet's harem. "Your goddess has need of your services. Come! *Worship her!*"

They do not hesitate.

Fallon is first, launching into the air. The others race to the stage, thundering toward me. Lust fills the air, hot and heavy.

Fallon moves behind me—I feel the heavy blow of his wings as he lands. The cross has my ass hanging just below the apex, and he grabs my hips, shifting me against the padding. His lubed cock slides into my ass, pressing hard as he thrusts up and in; his fingers dig into my hips, providing a focus for the sensation. Ari—better known as All-American Man, shifts to my front, taking the spot where Malcolm had been. With Fallon still in my ass, Ari thrusts up into my cunt, his cock pushing into my inner wall.

I am so *full* of cock.

Hazy-eyed, I look over Ari's shoulders to see Bryce, my Winter Warrior, riding his ass, creating one long line of cock with me at the center.

I gasp at the idea of it all, and then feel a cock in my mouth. Eyes streaming from strain and pleasure, I see the pale lights of a portal right above my face—the Doctor is using his powers to have me suck him off. I wrap my tongue around his cock, and hot, salty cum drips down my throat.

Good girl, Malcolm's voice whispers in my mind. *You are taking it all from all of them. Good girl.*

A cock in my ass, another in my pussy, another in my mouth.

More, I tell Malcolm with my mind. *More,* I demand.

I wiggle my fingers. The platform with the cross adjusts.

And then I feel the wet, slick folds in my palm. Using my powers, I see as Lillith mounts one of my hands and Piper the other. They rub their wet cunts into my palms, and they scream as I arch my fingers up, thrusting inside them as their own lovers thrust inside me. I use both thumbs to rub both women's clits, their own slick, hot wetness dribbling down my fingers.

Two others—my mind is too overridden with lust and sensation to comprehend who is doing what any more—two others start to suck on my bare toes, hands rubbing up my ankles, up my thighs, back down again.

Both of my breasts are being sucked, my nipples bitten, blood rushing all through my body.

Before, they took turns, like the simpering fools mortals too often are.

Now, they drink of me greedily, they do not wait, each one of them rushes to me, ramming their cocks into any hole they can find, rubbing their clits against me, sucking my skin and licking my moisture—sweat or cum, mine or theirs, they don't care. We are all consuming each other and being consumed and fucking, fucking, *fucking*, all of us, all at once, all on *me.*

I am a goddess, but in this moment, I have no power to do anything but accept the pleasure my worshippers bring to me.

And they bring it *all.*

My body is bound and raised, splayed and open, and they fill me. As one, they work together to shift, when one man is spent, another takes his spot. Orgasm after orgasm rolls off my body; I am already crescendoing into a new one before the throes of the first is done. My clit aches, but still a thumb rubs into it. My pussy clenches around one cock as it spurts inside me, and then it clenches around another that replaces the first. My ass is dripping, the passage slick and smooth as it's probed with fingers and cocks and toys. A sting of a whip across my legs; the kiss of a dozen lips over the bite.

I tip my head back to scream with pleasure after the Doctor releases his load down my throat, but I must swallow both his cum and my triumphant, joyous shout as someone's tongue caresses my lips in a hungry kiss. It leaves me gasping as those lips whirl away elsewhere, but then the sweet taste of a ripe cunt blossoms on my tongue. I probe that cunny with my teeth and tongue, finding the clit and swirling it against my bruised lips even as someone else rams me, hard, from both behind and in front, driving my face into the pussy.

And there—in the core of my being—I gather all this energy. It swirls inside me, pooling in my very core. Every orgasm that wracks my body adds to my power. Every orgasm I rip from theirs adds to my power.

I am a vessel—not just for their sexual pleasure, a depository of their cum and lust—no, I am a vessel for their *power*. It fills me; it overflows. My skin shivers and my body quakes but there is still more. More pussies, more cock, more *power*.

I am incandescent with it all.

12
MALCOLM

Sunlight streams through a gap in the curtains. I should get up, shift it closed so it doesn't wake her; but she has only recently stopped thrashing in restless sleep and fallen into an even unconsciousness, nestled under the crook of my arm as though it is my presence, my whole self curled around her that allows her this rest.

Far more likely it's due to the wild, insatiable fucking she endured, but for now, in the privacy of this bedroom with just us two, I will pretend it is me.

Persephone's face is pinched in this deep sleep, and I run my thumb over the crease between her brows until she sighs softly and the muscle relaxes. Christ, even that mere moan from her has my cock stirring again, stiffening sharply against her bent up knees.

She is too deeply asleep to feel it. She is too thoroughly exhausted. She needed the fucking last night;

but she needs rest, too, and so I will my body to calm, my desires to fade.

She is not mine to use, after all.

I am hers.

We are all hers, as I recognized last night. Every one of us mere mortals. We were always destined to be exactly as we ended up, panting and wound at her every desire. I am not even sure who all pleasured her, though I tried to keep count; I am not sure who I even ended up pleasuring, my own body taken over to the lust that emanated from her. But she was the core of anyone I fucked, the beacon, the sun.

She's always been the sun.

My sun.

I bend over and brush my lips across her forehead, breathing her in, feeling her softness under my mouth.

She has feasted now. And today, war awaits.

That makes my body stiffen in an entirely different way: with terror. Sheer and unrelenting.

Persephone has what she needs now, her power restored. Because of me? I think I must take the blame for it, and I will – oh, I will. Whatever happens to her in the coming days will be my doing, whether it be her survival or her death.

Just thinking those words.

Envisioning a world without her in it.

I press my lips more deeply to her skin, and though I know I should have restrained myself, she begins to stir. Without hesitation, she arches up and meets my hungry kisses, our lips tangling as our limbs entwine.

"It is morning," she whispers against me.

"You are not yet sated," I say, though we both know that isn't true. I let my cock have its way now, rising between us, probing the hot, wet center of her.

She bites her lip, smiles in a way that reminds me of when we first met, decades ago now. I didn't know who she was at first, just this fascinatingly gorgeous woman who happened to be at the same university as me.

And then she agreed to get coffee with me, and my world has revolved around her ever since.

Persephone shifts her hips, lets my cock slide just inside her entrance, teasing the tip. I groan, shocked at how quickly my own feral desire resets – I am exhausted and sore from last night, but I could ravish her utterly now–

She pulls away, leaving us both bothered and unsatisfied.

"We need to check on Gwen," she says.

"Scarlet has been giving me hourly updates," I say and tap my temple.

Persephone cocks an eyebrow. "You allow her into your mind?"

I pause. My head lulls onto the pillow, my eyes fixed on hers. "There is only one thing I fear now, and it is not your little mesmer toy invading my mind."

Persephone pushes up onto one elbow, looking

down at me. She doesn't have to ask; I push the image at her, the only thing I fear: losing her and Gwen. Her fighting Niberu, facing him as she inevitably will, and not walking away.

She leans down and kisses me again. This one is soft where we have had very little softness between us.

"It is morning," she says again, and I do nothing to counter her.

"I'M FINE. Really. Anthony's been taking good care of me."

I give her a flat stare and vehemently refuse to acknowledge the aforementioned man, who now sits beside Gwen's bed, also doing his damndest not to look at me.

Gwen shifts, scratching at her bandaged side. Her eyes are sunken, bruised; her face is gaunt with pain, and that alone has my hackles rising, my eyes flashing accusingly to Scarlet's nurse in the corner.

"Dad." Gwen snaps her fingers to get my attention. "Don't blame them. I refused the strongest pain pills – I want to be alert for this."

"Your only job now is to rest," Persephone says and she takes Gwen's hand, cradles it between her two.

My arm twitches. I'm standing behind Persephone, and I so badly want to reach out, take her shoulder; be part of this, be comforting.

I know my goal in the coming days: to keep her

alive. But I do not know how she wants me now. If she wants me. What will keep me in her good graces so I can stay close enough to keep her safe.

Gwen's eyes go from my face to my twitching hand and back.

I don't bother holding a mental block from her, from either of them, and after a moment, Gwen smirks and squeezes her mother's hand.

"The two of you seem to have…reconciled," Gwen starts.

Persephone doesn't look back at me. "In a way," is all she says.

Gwen's eyebrow goes up. "Ah. So I shouldn't–"

Both Persephone and Gwen freeze. I'm so focused on them that my mind only catches what has alerted them after a beat:

There's a new presence in Scarlet's base.

Lots of new presences.

I whirl to face the door just as Persephone launches up and grabs my arm. "Wait – it's all right."

Another beat, and I recognize the presences.

My eyes roll shut with something like a groan.

Lucas Gardson and a handful of Heroes from Heroes Org have just arrived.

Things have just gone from tense to…interesting.

"I'm going to go talk to him." Persephone turns back to Gwen and gives her a quick kiss on the forehead. "Rest. I'll be back soon."

"Can't he come here? I want to be part of this," Gwen says.

My chest bucks with refusal. *You're a child*, I want to say; but she isn't, not anymore, not for a long time.

She's *my* child still, though, and seeing her in this hospital bed, injured, pushes me into a war of conflict.

"Just rest," Persephone says, and she's out the door.

Gwen wilts in her mother's absence.

I bend to kiss her forehead too, but get halfway there when I realize maybe she doesn't want me to. She's likely not yet forgiven me for everything I did to her, the secrets I kept.

She sees my hesitation.

I settle for touching her hand and squeezing it once.

"Don't worry, love." I give her a wink and tap the side of my head. "You won't miss a thing."

Gwen cocks her head.

I open my mind to her, fully, my senses and sight and sound. She gasps a little at the breadth of it, but realization dawns in her eyes: I'll let her listen in on the conversation directly.

She smiles. It's true and bright and makes me immediately grin back at her.

"Thanks, Dad."

I squeeze her hand again. "For you, anything."

I'm out the door as Anthony asks what I did, and the two of them bend in quiet, intimate conversation. My parting glare at him doesn't hit home; he's too focused on my daughter.

That type of focus seems...familiar.

No time to think about it.

In the hall, I probe the surrounding minds of passersby – mostly still injured and medical staff – until I sense where Persephone has gone: to the landing bay.

There, the few planes Scarlet has are being prepped by still more busy hands, supplies loaded, fuel checked. A new arrival has some people unloading supplies, and I recognize a few of the faces now disembarking, all Heroes who served under my reign as CEO.

Their eyes meet mine as they scan the area. Again, the usual hatred, the sharp suspicion.

But when their new leader, Lucas, spots me and does nothing to retaliate, their hatred goes stagnant.

Lucas crosses the landing bay, a woman hot on his heels. Not just a woman: Rora, the daughter of Niberu himself.

I'd heard all about the new Heroes Org CEO's lover thanks to a particularly chatty guard while in Persephone's cell, but I still blink in shock at the Strachan woman, her vibrant green skin, her equally vibrant glare of ferocity. She's a force to be reckoned with, and she stands at Lucas's side unflinchingly as he meets Persephone in the middle of the landing bay.

I stride across the room just as Persephone and Lucas embrace.

"Brother," she says, deflating a little as he holds

her. She pulls back and grips his arms to survey the crowd behind him. "We didn't expect you for days at least."

"Ah. That was out of my control." Lucas's gaze flashes over Persephone's shoulder, to me, and back again swiftly. "I have brought reinforcements," he says instead of the explanation we all wait for.

Persephone surveys the Heroes briefly. "Yes," she starts. "I am glad for it. But–"

Lucas sighs. "There is no reasoning with humans. The Heroes Org board is firmly against any involvement with Niberu, save for what amounts to surrender. They hold that you give him the power gems so he will leave."

"He will not leave," Persephone states, deadpan.

Lucas pulls back to flare his hands helplessly. "I tried my best to reason with them, even after they unceremoniously ousted me from command. I tried to…persuade them. That only seemed to dig their mindset in deeper. So I borrowed what resources I could get my hands on–" He motions at the Heroes behind him. "And here we are."

Scarlet bursts into the landing bay, a door rebounding off the wall. At first, my chest bucks with panic that something has happened to Gwen, but I feel my daughter's presence in my mind still, watching, listening.

Scarlet hurries across the room, holding a pad in her hand. "You're going to want to see this," she tells

Persephone, and when she taps the screen, a video begins playing, a live stream of a news feed.

"Heroes Org has announced that the alien invaders are aligned with the infamous Villain Queen," a frazzled looking reporter says, shifting in her news chair. "They are amassing their forces to protect the public from this heinous threat. We go now live to the acting Heroes Org CEO."

The screen flashes to show a man I know well, one of the main brainless peons who populates the Heroes Org board.

"Christ, if *he's* acting CEO..." I start, voice trailing off.

Lucas gives me a *no shit, we're fucked* look, and I can't help but huff a brittle laugh.

"Heroes Org stands strong against all threats of villainy and evil," the man says. He's sweating, but his eyes blaze with a look of intense certainty; he really does believe this is all our fault. And maybe it is. "We formally condemn all Villains and demand that they cease this threat on our innocent population. Should they refuse, they will be met with the full force of our Heroes."

Lucas scoffs. "They have but half a dozen Heroes left. Most, once they learned the truth, opted to join me." He bats his hand at the crowd with him, all watching Scarlet's screen.

The newscast continues, but I've heard enough. I touch Persephone's arm, but her eyes aren't on the screen; they're on the floor, her mind lost in a whirl of thought.

I prod her mind, but she's locked down tight.

Still keeping me out.

After all these years, it shouldn't be surprising. It shouldn't hurt.

Why does it feel like my heart is breaking, then?

"What do you wish to do?" I whisper to her, barely stopping myself from adding *my queen.*

Persephone sniffs and looks up, her eyes level with her brother. "Call Thor here as well. He's still at his lover's laboratory. We need everyone, *everyone*, here, so we can prepare."

"Prepare for what?" It's Lucas who asks that, and I'm grateful, because while the question needs to be voiced, I don't want to ask it, don't want the answer.

Persephone hesitates. I'm still touching her arm, my fingers light on her skin.

After a pause, too long, too empty, she looks up at me.

There's fury in her eyes only. Fury at me. At what I will keep her from doing.

"For war," she says, and she pushes away. "Scarlet, with me," is her parting bark of command.

The newly arrived Heroes disperse, many offering to help the flurry of activity around them, others just sitting off to the side and letting their new realities sink in.

We're going to war.

It's happening. Finally. We plan a defense against Niberu, which will likely entail taking the fight to where he camps in the desert.

And there.

My love will be more vulnerable than she has ever been before.

She'll be fine, comes Gwen's still, soft voice, and I flinch. I'd forgotten I let her in so thoroughly.

Of course she will be, I tell her, because she *will* be. I'll see to it.

Then I shut Gwen out of my mind.

"I'd ask how my sister is," Lucas steps up to me, "but I think I know the answer."

My eyebrows raise. It's been so long since anyone has spoken to me without an obvious twist of derision or manipulation that it takes me a full breath to nod slowly at him.

Behind him, Rora is watching me curiously.

"Ever the queen," I say to Lucas.

"And you, ever her soldier," he cuts back.

I cock my head. Offense flares, but he's right. I am her soldier. I am her knight, her prince, her servant, whatever she needs of me.

I always have been.

My eyes drift out, lost in the spin and surge of terror, worry, strain. "Most of the time, I'm only her traitor."

"That's exactly what she needs."

I gape up at him, true surprise showing briefly on my face before I school my features.

Lucas squints. "You do know that your defiance is precisely what she needs? Or have you operated this whole time under the belief that your constant *butting of heads*, as the humans say, is detrimental to her? She feeds on your opposition simply because it is the only source of challenge she can trust. Unchecked, she will spiral, and lose herself; you have kept her grounded these past years in a way I have never seen from her." He steps closer to me and holds his hand out. "I know she hasn't nor will ever offer this, so I will. Thank you."

I stare stupidly at his outstretched hand.

Then I take it and he shakes slowly.

"Thank you," I say back, "for manning the helm of Heroes Org after my…ineffectual attempts at managerial reorganization."

Lucas barks laughter. Even Rora, still behind him, cuts a small smile.

"You did what I wanted to do every moment of every day at that godforsaken place," Lucas admits. "You should be sainted for not making all of their petty little minds melt out of their ears."

Now I laugh. Christ, it feels good. Foreign.

It feels how it must to have an ally.

"Eh, the war is young," I say, and Lucas swats my shoulder in something like camaraderie.

13
PERSEPHONE

Ships have launched, Scarlet informs me directly in my mind. She sends me an image from a satellite feed: more than half Niberu's fleet has dispersed, ships swarming like flies.

Where are they going? I ask her. She's several floors below me, in her observation room, and I'm striding down the hall towards my daughter's hospital bed.

Unknown, Scarlet answers. *But...* She sends me more images. Cities on the trajectories of the ships. New York. Chicago. Houston. Toronto. Mexico City. And beyond—London. Paris. Athens. Johannesburg. Moscow. Beijing. Tokyo.

Each one could be obliterated with only a ship or two.

But only if we don't fight back.

"That's the way of things, isn't it?" I say aloud. Malcolm is beside me again, as I knew he would be. I had felt him rushing to my side, his presence like a shield that floats around me, a buffer between me and the rest of the universe.

"What is the way of things?" Malcolm asks.

"Everything we love will be destroyed if we do not fight for it."

Malcolm grabs me by the arms, using my own purposeful strides as momentum to swing me around. "Love is not war," he says.

I take a breath, cupping his cheek. "Of course it is, darling," I say. And then I enter the hospital room of our daughter.

"Gwen?" I ask.

She's standing—shaky, but well enough for that. Anthony is nearby, holding her arm, but even as I watch, she steps away from him, standing on her own. Her spine is straight, her face tipped toward the light.

She is well, I think, relief making my mind relax its barriers.

She is, Malcolm's mind speaks back to mine, the joy blossoming around us.

But Gwen's strength falters. Anthony rushes for her elbow, steering her toward a chair by the window. She waves him off. "I'm fine, fine," she says. But her skin is ashen, her eyes dull. At least duller than normal. My gaze drifts up, following her eyes to the television mounted in the corner.

A news reporter stands in a boat in front of the Statue of Liberty. Just beyond Lady Liberty's crown, a half dozen of Niberu's spaceships hover, pointed at the city.

"We currently have confirmed that twenty of the world's largest cities are being threatened by this alien force," the reporter says, her vivid red hair flashing as she casts a worried look behind her. "The acting CEO of Heroes Org says that the ships are working at the behest of the Villain Queen, Persephone. No one currently knows of the Queen's location, nor has she reached out to negotiate a peace."

"There is no peace that can be negotiated," I say aloud through clenched teeth.

"The admiral of the alien force…" The reporter's voice trails off, and she touches her ear, listening to the earpiece. "The admiral's name is Nye-Bear-Rue," she states awkwardly. "He confirms that the Villain Queen stole from him, and he will retreat as soon as the items stolen are returned."

Malcolm snorts. We both know Niberu will only retreat after there's nothing left of Earth but ash.

"Anyone with any information on the Villain Queen's location *must* contact Heroes Org at the website or phone number displayed on your screen now." The reporter's voice cracks with fear, but it is misplaced.

She believes the lie Niberu has given her, given Earth. She believes that this is a simple case of a bad person stealing from a good person. That, after, we'll shake hands and all will be well.

Such simplicity in that lie, in the idea of good and evil being so clearly drawn as black and white lines.

How childlike Earth still is. I had known this, had I not? When they called me evil merely because I was the goddess of death, as if death were not simply the other side of life. Earth is so quick to believe that there are answers, if one looks in the right way, that there is truth in the binary, the dual.

For a moment I think of the orgy in Scarlet's harem. All the cock filling me up, my skin stretching to accommodate it all—it was painful, yes, but it was *good*. And there are plenty who would look at such acts and condemn them, but it does not matter; it was all still *good*.

I feel that goodness even now. My body feels too small, overflowing with the power pumping through me.

And then my eyes refocus, to the here, the now. They settle on Gwen. She watches me with a keen understanding. She has no care to know how much much my body must be filled for my power to likewise overflow, but she understands the way my hands curl into fists, the way my jaw clenches.

"I cannot lose this war," I say to her, to Malcolm, to myself. *Not again*, I add, this time so that only Malcolm can hear. He steps closer to me, wrapping his hand around mine until my fingers unwind from a fist and weave through his.

Before, in Asgard, when Niberu destroyed my home

world, my heart was set to fight. I was the goddess of death; I would kill him. But I had been fighting for that —for death.

And I had been weaker for it.

Now I fight for life. For Gwen's life. And Malcolm's. For all of Earth.

And there is much more power in that fight.

Malcolm squeezes my hand tighter, understanding the things I can not put into words. He leans in, kissing me gently on the lips, but that kiss grows needy, hungry.

"Ugh!" Gwen says, disgusted. "You guys! You're so gross!"

Anthony laughs, although the sound dies on his throat when Malcolm breaks the kiss long enough to glare at him. He may bring our daughter happiness, but Malcolm may never be able to forgive our daughter's lover.

I glance at Gwen. Despite pretending to be disgusted by her parents' love for each other, she's glowing inside, happy in a way I rarely see her. Malcolm's gaze drifts to her.

And it is their smile, reflected upon each other, that I will fight to the ends of the universe for.

14

MALCOLM

THE LANDING BAY IS PACKED WITH ACTIVITY, EVERY FREE hand not still tending to wounded enlisted to various tasks – starting the planes, prepping supplies, getting themselves ready. More than half of the people buzzing before me have powers of some sort that will come in useful in any fight. There is Fallon, his wings outstretched as Lillith fits him in a harness – she will stay here, assisting a team in Scarlet's lab manning the tech with others I've heard in passing, such as Thor's new lover, Daisy.

Speaking of, he has just arrived, and stands beside a man I will recognize: Ben Brand, more commonly known as the Wreck now, sits beside one of the cargo planes, looking like he's doing everything in his power to avoid breaking the supplies around him.

In the center of his chest, braced in a mighty harness, sits a power gem. It glows faintly, and for all its power it's all but lost against the massive threatening bulk of this creature. That is one of the three stones Niberu seeks to decimate whole worlds in a blink; he has another. Persephone has the last, though she has told no one where.

I shrug off the thought. It will not come to that. Without the three stones, Niberu is weak; we will destroy him long before they come into play, thanks to our own impressive arsenal.

The Wreck was meant to be one of my greatest weapons in the fight against Niberu. More beast than man.

Now, he will be, only a tool used by Persephone.

I should take comfort in knowing that, even in my failure, I still provided her a number of useful weapons. None of it is enough though; all of this activity, all of this preparation, it hardly matters, because I *did* fail. Had I succeeded in controlling all the assets of Heroes Org at my leisure, I would have been the sole general now marching out to face Niberu.

Not…her.

She is there, not more than three yards from me. I can't let her out of my sight. She goes over schematics with Scarlet and Daisy before Rora jogs up, asking for coordinates.

The people around her pause. Ah, that is the question still on everyone's mind – we prepare for war, but where will we make our final stand?

Persephone's lips part. Even with her mind

blocked from me – still; even with all the bridges crossed between us these past days, she keeps this reminder to me that I am at arm's length – I can feel her indecision. Which city will be the sacrificial battleground?

"Home," I say behind her.

She turns to look at me, as do Scarlet, Daisy, and Rora.

The sight of these four intensely powerful, smart women all fixated on me is not lost on my cock, which strains against my pants at the sight. I almost ask if Persephone needs another round in the harem before we go, but it is a stall tactic.

Persephone frowns at me. "Home?"

"LA."

Her eyebrows go up.

"We know the layout, we know how the city operates," I say. "Niberu may have satellite scans and recon, but he doesn't *know* that city, that terrain, like all these people do."

There's a pause before Scarlet nods slowly. "Home field advantage. It has positives."

"And negatives." But Persephone sighs. "Fine. Direct our forces to LA. We will make our stand against Niberu there. The moment he realizes I am on the battlefield, he will come, and–"

Here, her voice stops.

And...what?

I push the question at her. Demanding she answer.

She has said nothing of how she will defeat him. Of how this battle will culminate.

"And I will defeat him," she says simply. "We will defeat him. He is desperate and overconfident. He will fall."

But she sounds uncertain.

She sounds frightened.

Before I can think not to, I am taking her face in my hands and kissing her, hard, pushing my body against hers until she is forced to stand strong to avoid being walked backwards into Scarlet.

Persephone accepts my kiss – briefly. She pushes her hands on my chest and breaks apart from me, her eyes pinched in confusion, anger.

"Um…Daisy, Rora, let's go check on a few things," Scarlet says and whisks away the other two. Not that we're alone now, still in this overcrowded landing bay.

"You're staying here," Persephone says the moment they're gone.

I laugh. It's harsh. "No."

"Yes."

"If you lock me away, I will break out. I will find some way to you on my own and then you will have no control over me at all. Keeping me with you is better for everyone."

"*Malcolm.*" Persephone fists her hand in my shirt. I've changed, finally, thank God – now I'm in a far more acceptable white button up and slacks, hardly battle clothes, but no longer that awful prison uniform.

I think she took far too much pleasure seeing me in it.

"Besides," I say, reaching up to stroke my fingers along her cheek, "I am useful in situations like this, whether you want to admit it or not."

Persephone's lips press together. A grimace? I cannot tell.

"Gwen," she manages to say.

"There are others here to guard her, and this whole base is locked down tight. My place is with you." I lower my hand to hold her neck, thumb around her throat, feeling the bob and pulse of her heartbeat. "It always has been and always will be, and I'm afraid, my love, that there is nothing you can now do to remove me from your side."

Persephone gasps. I can't tell at first that it's a laugh, one strained by tears, until she looks up at me, and I see in her watery eyes an emotion I have not felt from her in years. Decades. Since I broke us. Since I destroyed everything.

"I love you," she tells me, and Christ, I am on fire.

I kiss her again. It's all I can do. It's all I'm meant to do, to serve this woman, to give her what she needs and let her take of me as she wills. But in moments like this, I am given all *I* need, all *I* want, filled to the brim with the waves of adoration and love she now lets me feel from her, her mind opening, a crack, a sliver. I dive headfirst into her love, cradling her face like the tender thing it is and exploring the inside of her mouth with my tongue. I will never tire of tracing its patterns, of absorbing her taste.

"I love you, too," I say into her, a promise, a worship.

Persephone pulls back from me, her breathing hard and heavy, and I know that if I push a little, I could coax her into bed.

"Let me prepare," she says, half begs it, and *Christ*, my achingly hard cock throbs.

I relent with a nod. "I'll be here."

She touches the center of my chest once more, her eyes there, where we connect, before she turns and walks off to one of the dozens of tasks she must complete in the next few moments.

I take a step after her before a pulse rocks in my mind. I recognize it and immediately open up to her.

The emotions I feel from Gwen are a mix of relief and joy, hesitation and happiness. We have dragged her through our war for far too long. She's right to be wary of our reconciliation.

We will do everything we can not to hurt you again, I tell her.

It's not me I'm worried about, she says, but she doesn't expand.

We'll both come back to you. I promise.
Dad?

I wait.

My attention goes to movement across the landing bay. Anthony has just entered, already dressed in his

Steel Soldier suit, minus the helmet, which he has tucked under his arm.

Immediately, my hackles raise.

Dad. Please, Gwen says. *I need to ask you something.*

Anything. Everything.

Keep him safe for me?

My chest kicks.

Anthony's eyes meet mine across the room. Instead of dipping away in fear, he holds, and after a long beat, he nods slowly.

I love him, Gwen tells me. *I know you hate him, but I love him. Please, please watch out for him. I hate that I won't be there, and I–*

She's crying. I hear her pause, the catch in even her thoughts.

Sweetheart, I cut her off. *I swear it. I'll keep him safe and bring him back to you, too.*

There's a moment of silence. Then a wash of relief, and I know she's crying again, crying at being stuck here while we go out without her, crying at the helplessness of it all.

We love you, I say. *And we will all come back to you.*

Promise? Her voice is a squeak, the little girl I used to sing to sleep after a nightmare.

I smile, eyes tearing. *I promise.*

15

PERSEPHONE

I seek out my brothers.

There are three of us that remain of the high royal family of Asgard. Me, Thor, and Loki.

It is fitting that the three of us go into battle together.

We are on different ships, flying from Scarlet's base to LA for the final defeat. I ride with Malcolm, Scarlet, and Fallon on a stealth jet. Loki is in a ship piloted by his lover, Rora. Thor heads to LA by ground, escorting the Wreck—it is too unsafe for the monstrous man to fly, but once they reach a certain point, Thor will use his portal for quicker transport.

I use my powers to speak to them privately just as the LA skyline comes into view. Niberu has stationed ten ships over the city; he guessed, I suppose, that we would come here. Niberu is always a few paces ahead of everyone else.

He expected us, Loki whispers in my mind.

I expected him, I answer.

These humans do not comprehend the full extent of his destructive rage, Thor says. I feel my brothers both mentally pause.

Are we enough? Thor asks, putting into words the fear all three of us have.

There is dark silence.

Niberu's ships turn to face my own. In the distance, I see black specks as more ships arrive, ready to fight.

Malcolm directs the jet we're on to head to the Heroes Org skyscraper. It is our rallying point, the tallest building in the city, the only beacon of hope. I hear, for a moment, the radio flick on, an enraged male voice demanding we leave Heroes Org flight space, and then Malcolm informs the radio operator to fuck off and severs all communication.

Brothers, I whisper, knowing they hear me. *You remember the plan that Mother and Father told us about, on Asgard?*

Hela, no, Thor tells me in my mind, using my old name, the name he called me when we were children. Loki does not answer, but I know he heard me. Thor tries to talk me out of the plan, tries to bargain with me, but Loki is silent.

That was always the way. Thor was ever optimistic, Loki was ever pessimistic. And me? I'm the realist. The one who saw the way things had to be, whether they were good or bad.

That's what death is, after all. It's not an evil thing, nor a good thing. It simply is.

I block both my brothers from my mind. I need neither Thor's pleading nor Loki's silence in this moment.

I know what I have to do.

My parents, after all, tried to do this to save Asgard.

But they didn't have a power gem.

I do.

Still...

I close my eyes, unsure whether I have the mental fortitude to do what must be done. It is a sacrifice, yes, one I have tried to prepare myself for, but not one I am ready—can be ready—to give. In the darkness behind my eyelids, I feel the jet hover into place. There is a crackle of energy throughout the city—portals opening, thanks to my followers with such powers.

Heroes and Villains alike stream into the city. Even as Niberu's ships dot the sky, more and more arriving each moment, my Heroes and Villains, united as one, come to fight.

To protect.

This world.

Each other.

I open my eyes.

"We are united," I say, the words escaping my lips.

Malcolm turns around and meets my eyes as the jet lands on the roof of the Heroes Org headquarters. "We are united for *you*," he says. It reminds me of the orgy, of the way everyone came—literally—to me. I am the center. The eye of the storm.

The calm before the rage.

"Let's go save the world," I say, and I step out of the ship.

Winds whip around me as I stride onto the rooftop—jets and helicopters docking here or nearby, plus the wild rush of portals opening. A bright purple portal rips through space and time to my right, and the Wreck strides out, the power gem strapped to his chest. Thor emerges after him, his eyes casting around before locking on me.

My brother rushes over to me. "You don't have to—" he starts, fear in his eyes.

I silence him with a look. "A last resort," I say. "A plan—"

"A sacrifice—"

"—that may save Earth." I roll my shoulders, meeting his eyes.

"What does that mean?" Malcolm says. His voice is wary, a line between his brows as he absorbs what was said, as well as what was not.

"You know me, darling," I whisper, dropping a kiss on his lips. "I always have another plan than the one you know about."

His frown deepens.

But overhead, a dozen more of Niberu's ships hover. They have identified our meeting point, and they spawn like demons above, ready to strike.

I turn to the Wreck. "Are you ready to obliterate them?"

He snarls, his eyes wilder than I have ever seen them, his massive fists like cinder blocks. He bends, smashing his fists into the rooftop, cracking the cement.

"Christ, hit the ships, not the building," Malcolm says.

Fortunately, Scarlet was able to hack the emergency response system, and every human with a cell phone has been alerted to evacuate. With the news showing the ships and the entire world of high alert, evacuations were surprisingly quick. No one was willing to fuck around with this threat.

The Wreck does not need to be told twice. He pounds over the rooftop, leaping up with a force I have never seen a mortal use, flying through the air and landing atop one of Niberu's ships. Before the ship can do more than dip and lurch at the added weight, the Wreck has cracked the top of the metal roof, peeling the steel away as if it were nothing more than tin foil. He reaches into the ship even as it spirals out of control, grabbing at the beings he finds inside and tossing them out of the ship. The bodies of Niberu's soldiers fall like confetti, smashing into the street thirty-five stories below. The ship spins out, but the Wreck uses its momentum to launch himself at another ship, doing the same.

"What are you doing just standing here?" Malcolm

bellows at the crowd around us. "This isn't a show. Attack! Attack!"

They do not need to be told twice.

The Heroes and Villains work as one. Those that can fly—Ari and Fallon with their bodies and Anthony with his suit, as well as a half dozen more powered beings—launch directly at the ships, as the Wreck did.

Thor gives me a salute with his hammer, then opens a portal directly inside one of Niberu's ships. He steps through, and it's not hard to see which ship he attacked —the one closest to the headquarters suddenly explodes from the inside, bodies of soldiers flying everywhere, with the cracking roar of Thor's hammer smashing before there's a glint of another portal, and another ship goes down.

Meanwhile, those who arrive in jets or spaceships, like Loki and Rora, turn their ships into a dogfight, drawing fire and leading Niberu's ships on a chase through the skys. We've scattered their ranks, ruined their perfect formation and planned attacks.

But there are more ships. More and more and more. With each one we take down, another arrives.

From my vantage point, I see two ships smash into each other, exploding like fireworks. I glance over at Malcolm.

"I have to contribute somehow," he says, smirking at me before turning his focus on two more.

Ah—my lover is using his mesmer powers to control the pilots of the ships, force them into an explosive suicide. But that will take a toll on him—controlling non-humans, pinpointing targets behind ships' shields. But Malcolm shows no sign of strain.

He is stronger than he was before.

We all are.

"Join me, my love!" Malcolm calls to me.

I smile at him.

Yes. Let them all see that I am the goddess of death.

I stand straight, reaching with my powers. Like little red threads, a thrum of life. The ships buzz—annoying flies. Inside them, I feel the lives of Niberu's soldiers. I wrap my fingers in those little threads, wind them around my palms, and I *pull.*

A dozen ships fall from the sky, but everyone inside them is already dead.

The sky is black with more and more of Niberu's fleet—all of them, I think, converging here, above us.

We are enormously outnumbered. They have *hundreds* of ships, thousands of soldiers.

But…

We have the Wreck, bouncing from ship to ship and breaking them each like children's toys.

We have Thor, smashing his hammer through portals and destroying the enemy from the inside.

We have All-American Man, hurtling his shield to deflect blasts.

We have the Steel Soldier, returning fire from the palms of his hands.

We have Malcolm, stealing the enemies' thoughts and using their own minds against them.

We have me.

And for the first time, I feel...

Hope.

AND THEN ONE more ship arrives. It soars through an enormous portal hovering over the sky.

This ship is unlike all the others. It's wider, stronger, with a phaser shield that's double layered. It gleams in the bright sun, and it has a hundred blaster cannons angled throughout the hull.

"Niberu," I whisper. I feel for the strand of his life. It's not weak like all the others. It's strong.

Unbreakable.

"Niberu," I say again, my voice cracking with fear.

16
MALCOLM

This is too easy.

The thought scratches at me, and I am ready to eviscerate whoever is letting doubt sneak into their thoughts around me – but then I realize.

It's me.

And it isn't the alien ships we're fighting that are too easy, no. Well, yes, but we are evenly matched, strain showing in our allies. What is too easy is where I stand currently, legs splayed on the roof of the Heroes Org building.

One weak chirp over the radio that we were *flying into their airspace*, then silence. We were not met with a rush of opposition the moment our armada touched down around this building; we are not beset by the buzz of cameras and news choppers.

The Heroes Org board just…conceded to our presence here. Not only that, but they are not seeking to *prove* that we are here, not twisting this battle against Niberu to their advantage in some blasphemous PR stunt.

As sure as I know Niberu will stop at nothing to get the destructive power gems, I know that the Heroes Org board members would use this situation to their benefit.

So something is wrong.

Out of the corner of my eye, I see Anthony finish off yet another ship. He whirls through midair, righting himself–

And like a shot, I react to the threat behind him before I even really see it: a missile launched at him from another ship.

I grab his mind – Christ, his mental defenses are shockingly weak; hasn't Gwen been training him? – and yank him, bodily, out of the air.

He tumbles down to the roof and lands in an unceremonious heap just yards from me.

The missile that had been aimed at him zooms over our heads before it slams into a different alien ship. Friendly fire.

Anthony pops the face shield of his helmet off and shoves to his feet. "What the hell–"

His eyes go to the smoking ship behind me and I watch as he follows the missile trail through the air to where he had been only moments ago.

"Oh." His cheeks are pink. "Thanks?"

"I need you to hack into the building," I tell him. "Find out why Heroes Org has been so silent."

Anthony hesitates, just a beat, before he nods. "Easy enough."

Easy enough? Many of the safety protocols in place were set up at my command–

Not important right now.

Anthony puts his face shield back on. It takes only a moment – maybe less – and in that time I spot Persephone again, only a yard or two from me. She had been focused on various ships, tearing lives out of bodies the way a butcher cleaves meat.

But now.

She is focused only on one ship.

One ship that descends, slowly, through a portal.

I don't need to reach out to feel whose presence is on that ship.

I don't need to throw my powers at it to feel the monstrosity within.

"Perse–" I start, her name tearing from me, but Anthony grabs my arm.

"We've got a problem," he says at the exact moment a blare of warning pierces through my skull. The same signal trumpets through our allies, whether in their heads or through an earpiece, and I feel us collectively hiss out a breath.

"Heroes Org is in play," comes a strained voice.

Lillith, back at Scarlet's base. "They've ordered a nuke strike on LA."

I cup my hands around my ears. Blocking out the sound of missiles firing and ships being ripped apart. "Come again?"

"A nuke strike," Anthony says in front of me.

I gape up at him.

He raises his face shield again, showing me the gaunt stretch of his features, helpless horror. "Heroes Org abandoned the building. There's no one here. Wherever they retreated to – I'm tracking them now – they've issued a nuke strike on the city."

My eyes leap to Niberu's ship. Persephone still faces off with it, neither of them moving as though they are trapped in their own reality while the battle around them is merely a dream.

"They know Niberu is here," I say to myself. "They waited to see where he'd pop up. Those fuckers. Those absolute *fuckers*."

I whirl towards Persephone and get close enough to touch her arm. My fingers extend, wrap around her bicep; I start to pull her, to drag her back onto our ship if we have to.

"Fall back–" I start to push the command at every ally I can grab, but Persephone seizes my arm, her relentless grip stopping me cold.

"No," she says, her gaze still fixed on Niberu's ship. "Let it come."

"Let–" My mind trips. "A *nuclear bomb* is coming at this city, Persephone. We can't–"

"I know." She still doesn't look at me. She just clings to me, and I feel the desperation in her grip, the tension in her fingers. "Let. It. Come."

17
PERSEPHONE

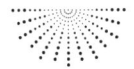

I knew this was a possibility.

I have always known.

Even a goddess must face her own mortality at some point.

And if death comes to the goddess of death? Well, there is some comfort in knowing that it will take both a nuclear explosion and the most bloodthirsty monster the universe has ever known to shuffle *me* off my mortal coil.

I feel Malcolm beside me, a sense in both my mind and heart. He is pleading—with me, with whatever god will listen—that I save myself.

But no.

Today is the day I save everyone else.

I see it all as if the action around me happens in slow motion, the players moving through fog, achingly paced. My allies, Hero and Villain alike, are unsure of how to react. Niberu's ship has dropped a hatch, and I see him, descending as if he has a right to this world, stepping out onto the open hangar, winds whipping his dark robes over his hulking body.

"Persephone," Malcolm says. "My love—"

I do not need his love in this moment. It has already filled me with power. Right now, I need his obedience.

Without taking my eyes from Niberu, I say, "Bring me the Wreck."

Malcolm snaps to attention. He understands an order when he hears one—that is, after all, what kept him in my bed and in my heart originally. Malcolm immediately calls over our radios for the Wreck to join us here, atop the Heroes Org building. I send out a mental summoning to Thor, who sees the Wreck as a brother. Thor knows that my summons will not harm his friend, but he still resists.

He knows what I plan to do to myself.

I brook no argument. My summons is not a negotiation.

My eyes do not leave Niberu. His ship draws closer, slowly, the clear command. Our allies stand down, an odd moment—mere seconds, truly—while the enemy enters, the final pieces fall into place, inevitability assumes its position.

The Wreck lands beside me with a cement-cracking thud. I hold my arm out, my palm open, my fingers grasping. The Wreck moves into position, and my right hand wraps around the power gem still harnessed to his chest plate.

I open my arms wide, my left hand pointing to Niberu. Wind whips my braids. He scans the city, the destruction already rendering buildings to ash, streets to debris.

And then his gaze meets mine.

We are close enough now that I can see the smile stretching over his horrific face. The smug glint in his eyes. The twist of his sneer that says, all too clearly, *I have already won.*

I grip the Wreck's power gem with my right hand and pull, breaking the sterlinium harness that had been around his chest. Bereft of the gem, he falls to his knees. Thor scoops him up, half-carrying, half-dragging him away.

"Persephone!" Malcolm's voice is choked with fear, and it's enough for me to glance at what he points to.

The nuclear missile, whizzing through the sky.

Toward Niberu, yes, but also toward *us.*

I whirl around, my left hand twirling. I summon the power gem from the portal dimension where I'd stashed it. It fills my palm.

Two gems. And me.

Against Niberu and a nuke.

I swing my arms together, my wrists smashing painfully into each other, the power gems in my hands forming the center of my fists. And I point it up, using my two index fingers as a target to seek out Niberu.

Over the whipping winds and the blasting phasers that have resumed fire around us, I hear Niberu shout.

"Do you really think that's enough?" There is mocking laughter in his words.

My fingers slip.

I point not to Niberu, but to the nuclear missile that is enough to level the entire city, but not, I think, enough to destroy Niberu.

I channel my power toward the nuclear missile.

It wobbles in the air. It had its own trajectory, and breaking that inertia, redirecting it in a slightly different angle—it is not easy. Or, it wouldn't have been, had I not held two of the three power gems.

I point the nuke to Niberu.

"Perse," Malcolm says. "If this—if this is the end—"

I cannot focus on saving everyone and sparing his heart. I know what Malcolm thinks.

A nuclear blast right at Niberu, this close, will kill us all.

He thinks I'm sacrificing everyone in LA, including him, to take down Niberu. But I'm not.

I'm just sacrificing myself.

Niberu flicks his hand, and a shield covers his ship even as the nuclear missile whistles closer. It's a deflector solar array with enough power to re-divert the missile, deflecting it off the shields so it bounces down to us. It's a strong enough shield that even as the nuclear missile leveled LA and all his armada, Niberu himself as his personal ship would be spared.

But I'm not going to let that happen.

I pull up my power—*all* of my power, from the very dregs of my strength—and I funnel it through the two gems in my hand. Niberu wears the crown, set with the one remaining power gem and two blank spaces where its mates are supposed to be inlaid. He adds his power gem to his shield.

But it is not enough.

The nuclear missile strikes the deflector solar array, and then I—I *stop* it. I don't let the nuke bounce off the shield. I hold it. I press it against the shield, and I *hold that motherfucker*.

Niberu's eyes widen slightly, watching.

I separate my palms, the power gems glittering in my hands. And I *push*.

Another shield, one of my own making, surrounds the nuclear missile. I have trapped Niberu with the missile.

And I *hold*.

I hold my shield up as his breaks.

I hold my shield up as the nuclear missile explodes.

I hold my shield up as his body is torn apart by the explosion, a mushroom cloud of destruction contained in the bubble radiating destructive power.

The city is spared. All I love is safe.

But within that shield—within the bloody haze of his own death—Niberu's power gem gleams.

He can never be truly killed as long as his power gem exists. His body will regenerate. His life is stored within his gem.

My brother Loki used almost all his magical force in an attempt to destroy the power gem in my right hand. Almost. It takes immortality to destroy immortality.

I have two gems. But even as I watch, driving all my power into the blast, I know it's not enough.

Not yet.

And so, I do the thing I thought I would never do.

I add my own immortality to the mix. I funnel every bit of power I have, including my godhood, through the two power gems in my hand, directed at the power gem already reforming the nuclear-exploded Niberu.

When my parents tried to face off against Niberu, back on Asgard, they sacrificed their immortality to protect us, but it hadn't been enough. It had spared a handful of our people, my brothers and I included, but it hadn't been enough. I have the power gems as well as my own immortality.

And that is enough.

Perhaps.

It drains from me. Immortality flows out of my body, adding more power to the gems I hold. The crystals start to crack. *Not yet. Not yet.*

I push every ounce of my own immortality, my own life force, into destroying Niberu's.

And with an explosion greater even than the nuclear blast, his power gem shatters.

Dust falls from my palms.

And then I, too, fall.

18
MALCOLM

The first explosion flattens everyone on the roof.

The second whips debris at us, rips the breath from my lungs, presses down on my chest when I try to claw to my feet.

"Persephone!"

The third explosion.

That one is from me.

That comes as I right onto my knees and see a form through the dust – faint, an outline, it punches me in the gut and I tear forward.

Nearby, I am aware of voices cheering. Niberu is defeated.

It comes through my comm unit, through my mental connection. *Niberu is defeated...carnage from his remaining ships...protect the innocents below the falling rubble–*

I block it. Block them.

This is no victory.

She is lying on the roof, her hands out before her, a glittering dust in her scorched palms. Her eyes are closed.

"Persephone," I say her name as a command, because this is not how it will end, *this is not*. I grab her shoulder and heave her onto her back, my hand going to her neck, feeling for a pulse.

Nothing.

Nothing.

A second longer, just a second longer–

Nothing.

I refuse this reality. My powers funnel out, seeking solution, feeling the minds of all around me and their mix of pain, joy, and fear. In them I find nothing that could help, nothing that could undo what has been done, and I gather Persephone to my chest, shaking.

No.

I was supposed to stop her. I was supposed to *protect* her where she wouldn't protect herself, and though I know this is what she wanted, this is the end she would have chosen, I am rage incarnate.

A hand touches my shoulder. "Malcolm–"

It is Loki, and with him, Thor, and they are gaunt and teary-eyed and shocked and I hate them as powerfully as I hate myself.

Desperation tears through me and I look down at Persephone's face. She looks…at peace.

No.

I kiss her. I push my mouth to hers ferociously, because there is nothing else I can do. All my power, all my rage, all my love and hurt and terror and anger – none of it can do a damn thing in the face of my love's one act.

She saved us.

And I couldn't save her.

I hold there against her, breathing in the sweat and stench of battle, the air gritty with dust.

And then, as I should have done every moment she was alive, I pray, "Come back."

She is a goddess, she is *my* goddess, and I pour my worship onto her, giving her every feeble part of me.

In my arms.

Against my chest.

She stirs.

I go rigid. Has my mind broken? Have I–

Again, she moves, and when I pull away from her lips, she rocks back with a gasp, eyes flying open.

Relief is cool and bright and resilient. I moan, tears surging down my cheeks, and I cling more tightly to her until she settles, her breathing going from panicked to even. Her eyes, her *eyes*, they are open and locked on me and filling with tears.

"Malcolm – what –"

Her focus goes to the smoking sky around us. In that sky hover our allies, whether on ships or flying, all attention on us, on her.

They see her upright, *alive*, and their cheers are deafening.

I arch into her, my forehead to her shoulder, drained, suddenly. Did I bring her back from the afterlife? I do not question it.

I am merely here, feeling her against me, and I am undone.

Persephone wraps her arms around me. "Malcolm," she says into my neck and then she finds my mouth, and I cup her head to kiss her properly.

"You did it," I whisper into her. I should berate her for what she did, what she put me through. I might have, had I not seen her make this sacrifice. Her power is so far beyond anything I can comprehend. This woman, this goddess, is above us all, and I am content now to bask in her presence.

"I did," she says, and she strokes a finger down my cheek. "I did it for you. For Gwen. For us."

"My queen," I say, and kiss her again. "My goddess."

Around us, our allies cheer.

Above us, the dust breaks, and a beam of sunlight shines through.

Anthony finds the Heroes Org board hiding in a bunker in Montana.

Most are battered and wounded, but a few eagerly tag along. Myself, Anthony; Loki and Rora; the Wreck and Daisy; Ari, Bryce, Piper. Lillith stays behind, but sends us off with a message to make sure the Heroes Org board is watching the news.

Ominous, but I don't question it, and we descend on that bunker with terror only – no intent to kill, despite what my rage requires. Ari is, as ever, the voice of reason, holding us back from doing more than obliterating their weak little tin can of a hideout and dragging them into the evening light.

Loki turns on the news in his ship and at the base of the open loading bay, we watch as a flustered news reporter recaps events.

Turns out there *were* cameras watching us in LA.

Only cameras controlled by Scarlet and Lillith.

Scenes flash across the screen. Our fight, Niberu's ship, his aliens – and, most notably, the nuclear bomb.

"Reports are coming in that the bomb's origins can be traced to a hideout owned by Heroes Org," says the reporter. Her face goes slack with horror. "They…is that correct? We– we have to confirm this, but breaking news: Heroes Org ordered a nuclear attack against a US city–"

The board members hang their heads, made to kneel on the dead grass. They say nothing. Wisely.

As we load them onto the ship, I'm perhaps a bit too rough with one of them.

"Well," I say, heaving the man into the holding cell so he rebounds off the metal wall. "I guess crime doesn't pay."

Next to me, Anthony gives me a wide-eyed look of…humor?

I frown at him. "What?"

He laughs. "I can't believe you just said that. That's the most *dad* thing I've ever heard and, in this, moment I swear I finally just accepted you as Gwen's father."

I should be offended. I should remind him of what I am and what I can do.

Instead, I smile back.

EPILOGUE

PERSEPHONE

I CHOSE A NEW ISLAND. It's in the Pacific, uncharted. It had been nothing more than volcanic rock, but when you have supers on your side, anything can be turned into a paradise.

And that's what this is.

I call it Eden, a garden of knowledge and plenty where clothes are assuredly optional. I do not build a castle. I no longer need nor want a fortress.

I build a home.

My daughter comes up to me with a bouquet of tropical flowers in her hands. "Mom," she says flatly, looking up at the cloud-speckled sky. "You have to wear something to your own wedding. A dress preferably, but I'll take a pantsuit. A bikini. Fig leaves? Literally anything."

"Darling, you're such a prude."

"Mother, you're such a nude...ist. That sounded better in my head."

I wave my hands as I stand, a simple white silk gown draping my curves. Gwen *finally* looks at me. She rarely stays on my island with me, despite there being enough room for anyone and everyone—it's easy to expand a tropical paradise when one has portals.

I suppose it is somewhat awkward for my daughter and her lover to be under the gaze of her parents. I shrug. Earth is still very different from Asgard.

But at least it's safe now.

Gwen thrusts the flowers into my hands. She's a little wobbly, and I reach out on instinct, taking her elbow. Her belly has only just begun to round, a soft little bulge. Gwen's hand splays over her middle.

A daughter, I think, reaching out with my powers. I don't tell Gwen—I don't want to ruin the discovery of her daughter for her because I know she's purposefully blocked her mind from her child's, hoping for the surprise—but I cannot help but feel the private joy of our line continuing. She will be strong like me. Like her mother.

And Malcolm will be beside himself with joy.

"Why do we even need flowers?" I ask as Gwen and I walk, arm in arm, through the lush, dense tropical forest. Winding paths lined with hibiscus flowers lead us toward the beach.

"It's a wedding, Mom." Gwen sounds confused.

"An Earth tradition."

"A ceremony," Gwen says. "An excuse for a party. We can all use something to celebrate."

"Can we not simply celebrate our planet's survival?" It has been months, but the entire world still seems heady with joy. Every human on this world saw—for a moment—the fleeting nature of their world.

And they also saw that there were those willing to give all to save it. Hero and Villain.

United.

Perhaps this marriage ceremony isn't such a bad idea.

The palm trees give way to a sandy beach. Our friends are all there—Ari and his lovers, Lillith and Fallon, Scarlet and Watcher. Everyone here. Everyone in love.

To celebrate my love.

I am used to feeding off of sexual energy and emotion because it's an easy high to chase. An orgasm is an orgasm, and it fills me up quickly and well. But the trueness of this love—it fills me in a different way, a way, I think, that will sustain me longer.

At the end of the rows of people, standing alone, inches from the waves gently rolling in—stands my love.

He watches me, love and a hint of worry in his eyes. As if he feared I would not come.

I will always come, I tell him in my mind.

From the smirk that twists his lips, I know he's come up with an alternative meaning of that word.

Gwen, not privy to her father's mind in this moment, gives my arm a squeeze and then lets me continue to Malcolm on my own. When I reach him, I turn to look back at the home I've made, the friends I've fought with, the daughter I love.

When I defeated Niberu, I gave up my mortality.

This, now, is my forever. I shall grow old beside Malcolm, as he grows old beside me. We shall value this daughter, this granddaughter, all who come to our lives.

We shall be in love.

Compared to immortality, it may seem like a little life.

But there is a forever to our love that cannot be contained by the flimsy walls of mortality.

I put my hand in his.

And I welcome forever.

19
MORE

THANK YOU

Sincerely, thank you so much for joining us on this adventure! Liza and Natasha started writing these books for fun, and they evolved into an epic tale almost as worthy as the heroes and villains that inspired them. But we could not have done it without you. Thank you for reading, for reviewing, for cheering us on with social media, for subscribing to our newsletter. Thank you, thank you, thank you.

WE HOPE you join us for what we have next—we're deep at work planning our next super sexy series with bigger-than-life characters. If you want to be the first to find out about our new series, subscribe to our newsletter at: rarebooks.substack.com.

. . .

Meanwhile, be sure to read Natasha and Liza's other works! If you're a fan of superhero movies (which, we assume you *are* since you're here and our kind of people!), you must check out Natasha's Celebrity Crush series—it's basically what the stars of the movies do behind the scenes, and it is ultra spicy! Start with *Meet Cute,* featuring celebrity Tom and the diner waitress that has him going way off-script. Quick and steamy, these books are pure fun (in more ways than one!)

Liza has been working on *As Above*, a romantic fantasy serial novel. Empress Elenka thinks her life is perfect after a prophecy leads to her marriage to the Sky Emperor. But this court is full of lies and subterfuge, and if she wants to protect humanity, she cannot simply be a pretty, ornamental wife. The more she acts, though, the closer to danger she comes…especially when the most powerful god in the lands chooses to put her aside for another bride, one more pliable and more capable of giving him the kingdom he wants. With twists you won't see coming, this serialized novel explores all the realms (and, spoiler: Liza's absolutely taking Elenka to the Underworld before this is all done!).

Again, thank you for reading and supporting us! Keep up with these and all our latest books (plus freebies!) by subscribing to our newsletter at: rarebooks.substack.com.

ABOUT THE AUTHORS

Liza Penn and Natasha Luxe are a pair of author friends with bestselling books under different names. They joined forces—like all the best superheroes do—for the greater good.

You can keep up with them at their newsletter. Located at http://rarebooks.substack.com, they often feature links to freebies and bonus material.

For more information about all their books and extra goodies for readers, check out their website at thepennandluxe.com.

ALSO BY LIZA PENN & NATASHA LUXE

THE HEROES AND VILLAINS SERIES:
All books also available in paperback

Prequel Novella: Origin (*free for subscribers*)
Book 1: Nemesis
Newsletter short story "Fly With Us"
Book 2: Alter Ego
Book 3: Secret Sanctum

Bundled Box Set of Books 1-3 + Novella Origin

Book 4: Magician
Book 5: Thunder
Book 6: Goddess

ALSO BY NATASHA LUXE
Celebrity Crush Series

ALSO BY LIZA PENN:
As Above Romance Fantasy Serial
Hotel Ever After Series

Printed in Great Britain
by Amazon